THE HAUNTED MONASTERY

ROBERT VAN GULIK

THE HAUNTED MONASTERY

A Judge Dee Mystery

With eight illustrations
drawn by the author in Chinese style

THE UNIVERSITY OF CHICAGO PRESS

The University of Chicago Press, Chicago 60637

University of Chicago Press Edition 1997
Printed in the United States of America
16 15 14 13 12 11 10   3 4 5 6
ISBN-13: 978-0-226-84879-2 (paper)
ISBN-10: 0-226-84879-5 (paper)

Library of Congress Cataloging-in-Publication Data

Gulik, Robert Hans van, 1910–1967.
The haunted monastery / Robert Van Gulik.
p.   cm. — (A Judge Dee mystery)
ISBN 0-226-84879-5 (alk. paper)
1. Dee Jen-Djieh (Fictitious character) —
Fiction.   2. China — History — T'ang dynasty,
618–907—Fiction. 3 Judges—China—Fiction.
I. Title. II. Series: Gulik, Robert Hans van,
1910–1967.   Judge Dee mystery.
PR9130.9.G8H38 1997
823' .914—dc21   96-53138
                                                              CIP

Illustrations

A diagram of the monastery will be found on page 72, and a more detailed sketch on page viii.

Dramatis Personae

Note that in Chinese the surname – here printed in capitals – precedes the personal name

Main characters
DEE Jen-djieh. Magistrate of Han-yuan, the mountain district where the Monastery of the Morning Clouds is located
TAO Gan. One of Judge Dee's lieutenants

Persons connected with 'The Case of the Embalmed Abbot'
True Wisdom. Abbot of the Monastery of the Morning Clouds
Jade Mirror. Former Abbot of the same monastery
SUN Ming. A Taoist sage, former Imperial Tutor, who lives retired in the monastery

Persons connected with 'The Case of the Pious Maid'
Mrs PAO. A widow from the capital
White Rose. Her daughter
TSUNG Lee. A poet

Persons connected with 'The Case of the Morose Monk'
KUAN Lai. Director of a theatrical troupe
Miss TING. An actress
Miss OU-YANG. An actress
MO Mo-te. An actor

Sketch Map of the Monastery

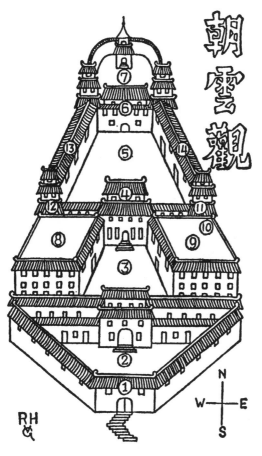

朝
雲
觀

N
W — E
S

1

The two men sitting close together in the secluded room, up in the tower of the old monastery, listened for a while silently to the roar of the storm that was raging among the dark mountains outside. Violent gusts of wind were tearing at the tower, the cold draught penetrated even the solid wooden shutters.

One of the men looked uneasily at the flickering flame of the single candle that cast their two weirdly distorted shadows on the plaster wall. He asked again in a tired voice:

'Why do you insist on doing it tonight?'

'Because I choose to!' the second replied placidly. 'Don't you think that today's feast is a most appropriate occasion?'

'With all those people about here?' the first asked dubiously.

'You are not afraid, are you?' his companion asked with a sneer. 'You weren't afraid on that former occasion, remember?'

The other made no reply. Thunder rumbled in the distant mountains. Then there came a torrential downpour. The rain clattered against the shutters with a rattle as of hailstones. Suddenly he said:

'No, I am not afraid. But I repeat that the face

of the morose fellow looks familiar to me. It worries me that I can't remember when or where I . . .'

'You distress me!' the man opposite him interrupted with mock politeness.

The first frowned, then resumed:

'I wish you wouldn't kill her, this time. People might remember, and start wondering why three . . .'

'It all depends on her herself, doesn't it?' His thin lips curved in a cruel smile. Rising abruptly, he added: 'Let's go back, they'll notice our absence in the hall below. We must never forget to act our parts, my friend!'

The other got up also. He muttered something but his words were drowned in another roll of thunder. It seemed very near, this time.

2

Farther down in the mountains on the southern border of Hanyuan, that thunderclap made Judge Dee lift his head in the pouring rain and anxiously inspect the dark, windswept sky. He pressed himself close to the side of the high tilt-cart, drawn up under the cliff that overhung the mountain road. Wiping the rain from his eyes he said to the two coachmen who stood before him huddled in their straw rain-cloaks:

'Since we can't go on to Han-yuan this evening, we'd better pass the night right here in our cart. You could fetch some rice for our evening meal from a farm in the neighbourhood, I suppose?'

The elder coachman pulled the piece of oil-cloth closer to his head, the ends were flapping in the strong wind. He said:

'It isn't safe to stay here, sir! I know these autumn storms in the mountains, it's only just beginning! Soon there'll be a real gale. It might blow our cart over into the ravine on the other side of the road.'

'We are high up in the mountains,' the other coachman added. 'There is not a hut or farm for miles around, there's only the old monastery up there. But of course you wouldn't like to . . .'

A flash of lightning lit up the wild mountain

scene. For one brief moment Judge Dee saw the high, scraggy mountains that loomed on all sides, and the red mass of the old monastery, towering on the slope above them, on the other side of the ravine. There was a deafening clap of thunder, and all was dark again.

The judge hesitated. He pushed his long black beard farther into the fold of his drenched travelling-cloak. Then he made a decision.

'You two run up to the monastery,' he said curtly, 'and tell them that the magistrate of this district is here and wants to stay overnight. Let them send down a dozen lay brothers with closed litters, to carry my womenfolk and luggage up there.' The elder coachman wanted to say something, but Judge Dee barked: 'Get going!'

The man shrugged his shoulders resignedly. They set off at a trot, their storm lanterns of oiled paper were two dancing spots of light in the dark.

Judge Dee felt his way along the tilt-cart till he found the stepladder. He climbed inside and quickly closed the canvas flap behind him. His three wives were sitting on the bed-rolls, their padded travelling-cloaks drawn close to their bodies. In the back of the cart the maids cowered among the bags and boxes. Their faces white with fear, they pressed close to each other at each peal of thunder. It was dry inside, but the cold wind blew right through the thick canvas of the hood.

As the judge sat down on a clothes box his First Lady said: 'You shouldn't have gone outside! You are wet through and through!'

4

'I tried to help Tao Gan and the coachmen to fix that broken axle,' he said with a wan smile, 'but it's no use, it'll have to be replaced. Anyway, the horses are tired and the storm is only beginning. We'll stay the night in the Morning Cloud Monastery, that's the only inhabited place in this neighbourhood.'

'Do you mean that huge red building with the green-tiled roofs we saw high up on the mountain slope, when we passed here two weeks ago?' his second wife asked.

The judge nodded.

'You won't be too uncomfortable there,' he said. 'It's the largest Taoist monastery in the entire province, and many people visit it during the religious feasts. I am sure they'll have good guest quarters.'

He took the towel his third wife gave him and tried to rub his beard and whiskers dry.

'We'll manage all right!' his First Lady resumed. 'During our holiday in the capital we were so spoilt in your uncle's mansion that a little hardship won't matter! And it'll be interesting to see what that old monastery looks like inside!'

'Perhaps there are spooks!' his Third Lady said with a smile. She moved her shapely shoulders in an exaggerated shudder.

Judge Dee knitted his thick eyebrows.

'There isn't much to see,' he said slowly. 'It's just an old monastery. We'll have the evening meal in our room and go to bed early. If we leave tomorrow morning at dawn, as soon as the grooms of the monastery have replaced the axle, we'll be back in Han-yuan before the noon rice.'

'I wonder how the children have been getting along!' his second wife said in a worried voice.

'Old Hoong and the steward will have looked after them,' the judge said reassuringly. They talked about household matters till loud shouts outside announced the arrival of the men from the monastery. Tao Gan, one of Judge Dee's lieutenants, poked his long, gloomy face inside and reported that four litters were standing ready for the ladies.

While Judge Dee's three wives and their maids got into the litters, the judge and Tao Gan supervised the lay brothers as they rolled large boulders up against the wheels of the cart. The coachmen unharnessed the horses, and the cortège moved along the winding road, the rain clattering on the canvas roofs of the litters. Judge Dee and Tao Gan trudged along behind them – they were drenched to the skin anyway! In this strong wind it was no use trying to unfold their oil-paper umbrellas.

As they were crossing the natural bridge over the ravine, Tao Gan asked:

'Isn't that the monastery which Your Honour planned to visit some time ago, in order to make inquiries about those three young women, called Liu, Huang and Gao, who died there last year?'

'It is,' the judge replied soberly. 'It's not the kind of place where I would choose to stay overnight together with my womenfolk. But it can't be helped.'

6

The sure-footed litter-bearers went quickly up a steep flight of slippery steps, zig-zagging up through high trees. Judge Dee followed close behind them but he found it difficult to keep up with their pace. He was glad when, above him, he heard a gate open on creaking hinges. They entered a large, walled-in front courtyard.

The bearers carried the litters up a second flight of steps at the back of the court, and put them down under a high archway of blackened bricks. A group of monks in saffron-coloured robes stood waiting for them there, carrying lampions and smoking torches.

Judge Dee heard the main gate through which they had entered close with a resounding thud. He suddenly shivered. He thought he must have caught a bad cold in the rain. A short, corpulent monk stepped forward and bowed deeply in front of him. He said in a brisk voice:

'Welcome to the Morning Cloud Monastery, Your Honour! I am the Prior here, at Your Honour's service!'

'I hope our sudden visit didn't inconvenience you,' Judge Dee said politely.

'It's a signal honour, sir!' the Prior exclaimed, blinking his slightly protruding eyes. 'It adds splendour to this auspicious day! We are celebrating the foundation of our monastery, as we do every year on this day. This is the two hundred and third time, Your Honour!'

'I didn't know that,' the judge said. 'May your monastery prosper for ever and ever!' A gust of cold wind blew through the archway. He cast an anxious eye at his ladies, who were stepping down from the litters, assisted by the maids, and resumed: 'Please lead us to our quarters. We all need to change our clothes.'

'Of course, of course!' the small Prior exclaimed. 'Follow me, please!' As he led them into a narrow, dark passage he continued: 'I hope you won't mind the steps. I'll take you to the east wing by a roundabout way. There are many sets of steps, but it'll at least save you from going outside again and getting more wet!'

He went ahead, holding a paper lantern close to the floor so that Judge Dee and Tao Gan could see the steps. A novice followed, carrying a lampion on a long stick, and Judge Dee's wives brought up the rear, together with six lay brothers, who carried their travelling bags and boxes, suspended on bamboo poles over their shoulders. When they had gone up the first flight of stairs and turned a corner, it had grown very still; nothing was heard any more of the storm outside.

'The walls must be very thick!' Judge Dee remarked to Tao Gan.

'They knew how to build in those days! And they didn't grudge expense!' As they began another steep ascent, Tao Gan added: 'But they made far too many stairs!'

After they had climbed two more flights of stairs, the Prior pushed a heavy door open. They entered a long, cold corridor, lighted by a few lanterns hanging from the thick, age-blackened rafters overhead. On their right was a blind plaster-wall, on the left was a row of narrow, high windows. Here they heard again the gale blowing outside.

'We are now on the third floor of the east wing,' the Prior explained. 'The steps on the left there lead down to the hall on the ground floor. If Your Honour listens you can hear faintly the music of the mystery play they are performing there now!'

The judge halted and listened politely. He could vaguely hear the beat of drums coming from far below. It was soon drowned by the rattle of the rain against the shutters. The wind was gaining in force. He was glad they were inside.

'Round the corner ahead there,' the Prior went on in his quick, clipped voice, 'are Your Honour's quarters. I trust you won't find them too uncomfortable. Presently I'll take Your Honour's assistant down to his room on the floor below, where we have a few other guests staying.' He motioned the novice with the lampion to precede them, and they went on.

Judge Dee looked round. His wives and the maids were just emerging at the head of the stairs at the end of the corridor. He followed the Prior.

Suddenly a particularly violent rush of wind blew open the shutters of the window on his left, and a gust of cold rain came inside. With an annoyed exclamation Judge Dee leaned outside and grabbed the swinging shutters to pull them shut. But then he stood stock-still.

The window in the wall of the building opposite

stood open; across the dividing space of six feet or so he looked into a dimly-lit room. He saw the broad back of a man wearing a close-fitting iron helmet who was trying to embrace a naked woman. She covered her face with her right arm, where the left should have been there was only a ragged stump. The man let go of her and she stumbled back against the wall. Then the wind tore the hooks of the shutters from Judge Dee's hands, and they slammed shut in his face. With an oath he pushed them open again, but now he saw nothing but a dark curtain of rain.

By the time he had the shutters fastened, Tao Gan and the Prior had stepped up to him and helped him to secure the rusty bolts.

'You should have let me do that, Your Honour!' the Prior said contritely.

The judge remained silent. He waited till the women and the bearers had passed by them, then asked:

'What is that building over on the other side there?'

'Only the store-room, Your Honour,' the Prior replied. 'We had better . . .'

'Just now I saw one of the windows there standing open,' Judge Dee interrupted him curtly. 'But someone closed it very quickly.'

'Window?' the Prior asked astonished. 'Your Honour must be mistaken! There are no windows on this side of the store-room. There's only a blind wall. This way please!'

3

Silently Judge Dee followed him round the corner. There was a dull pain behind his eyes, evidently he had caught a head cold. Moreover, he had been looking through the grey curtain of the falling rain, and it had been only one brief glance. He felt feverish, it could have been a hallucination. He gave Tao Gan a quick look, but apparently his assistant had seen nothing. He said:

'You had better go and change, Tao Gan! Come back here as soon as you are ready.'

The Prior took his leave with many bows. He walked back to the stairs together with Tao Gan.

In the spacious dressing-room his First Lady was giving directions to the maids as to which of their boxes should be opened. His two other wives were supervising the bearers, who were busy filling the bronze brazier with glowing coals. The judge looked on for a while, then walked on to the bedroom beyond.

It was a very large room with only a few pieces of solid, old-fashioned furniture. Although thick draperies were drawn over the windows, he could hear faintly the sounds of the storm outside. A huge bedstead stood against the back wall, heavy curtains of antique brocade hung down from its carved ebony canopy, high up near the raftered ceiling. In the corner he saw a dressing-table of blackwood, and next to it a small tea-table with four stools. Except for a large bronze brazier there was no other furniture. The floor was covered by a thick, faded brown carpet. The room didn't seem very inviting, but he reflected that when the brazier was burning and all the candles lighted it would probably not be too bad.

He pulled the curtains of the bedstead aside. It provided ample room for himself and his three wives. As a rule he didn't like them all sleeping together. At home each of his wives had her own separate bedroom, and he either passed the night there or invited one to his own bedroom. As a staunch Confucianist he thought that to be the only proper arrangement. He knew that many husbands slept with all their wives together in one bedroom, but Judge Dee thought that a bad habit. It lessened the women's self-respect and did not make for a harmonious household. However, when travelling it couldn't be helped. He went back to the dressing-room, and sneezed several times.

'Here's a nice padded robe for you!' his First Lady said. And, softer: 'Do I give a tip to those lay brothers?'

'Better not,' the judge whispered. 'We'll leave a gift to the monastery when we take our departure tomorrow.' Louder, he added: 'That robe'll do!'

His second wife helped him to change into the dry garments after having warmed them over the brazier.

The First Lady Directs the Maids

'Give me my new cap!' Judge Dee said to his First Lady. 'I'll have to go down now and say a few polite things to the Abbot.'

'Come back here quickly, please,' she said. 'We'll make some hot tea, then have our meal here. You had better get to bed early, you are looking pale. I think you have a cold coming on!'

'I'll be up as soon as I can,' Judge Dee promised. 'You are right, I don't feel too well. I must have caught a bad cold.' He tied the black sash round his waist, then his ladies conducted him to the door.

Tao Gan was waiting for the judge in the corridor, together with the novice carrying a lampion. His gaunt assistant had changed into a long gown of faded blue cloth, and he had a small square cap of well-worn black velvet on his head.

'The Abbot is waiting for Your Honour in the reception room downstairs,' the novice said respectfully when they were entering the corridor that led to the staircase. Judge Dee halted in his steps. He said:

'We'll go there presently.'

He stood listening for a while. The sound of the rain seemed less than before. He unfastened the shutters of the window through which he had seen the weird scene. Only a little rain blew in from the darkness outside. He saw a solid brick wall directly in front of him. Higher up there were two windows of a tower; below the blind wall continued into the deep well that separated the two buildings. Thunder rumbled again. He closed the window and remarked casually to the novice:

'Beastly weather! Lead us now to the store-room opposite here!'

The novice gave him an astonished look. He said doubtfully:

'We'll have to go a long way, sir! We must first descend two floors to get to the passage that connects the two buildings, then we must go up again two – '

'Lead the way!' Judge Dee ordered curtly.

Tao Gan gave the judge a curious look. Seeing his impassive face, however, he refrained from asking the question that was on his lips.

They descended the dark stairs in silence. The novice led them through a narrow passage, then they went up a steep staircase. On top was a landing, surrounding a large square well. The heavy scent of Indian incense wafted up through the lattice-work screen that lined the well on all four sides.

'Deep down there is the nave of the monastery's temple,' the novice explained. 'Here we are on the same level as Your Honour's floor in the east wing.' Entering a long, narrow corridor he added: 'This leads to the store-room.'

Judge Dee stood still. Smoothing down his long black beard he looked at the three high windows in the plaster wall on his right. Their sills were only about two feet above the floor.

The novice had pushed a heavy door open. He preceded the two men into an oblong, low-ceilinged room. The light of two candles shone on piles of boxes and bundles.

'Why are those candles burning here?' the judge asked.

'The monks go in and out of here all the time, sir, to fetch the masks and the stage dresses,' the novice replied. He pointed at the row of large wooden masks and gorgeous brocade robes that covered the wall on their left. The wall on the right was taken up entirely by a wooden rack, stacked with halberds, spears, tridents, flagpoles and other paraphernalia used in the mystery plays. The judge noticed that neither wall had a single window, there were only two small ones in the back wall opposite them. He estimated that those two windows must be facing east, in the outer wall of the monastery. He turned to the novice and said:

'Wait for us outside!'

Tao Gan had been surveying the room, pensively playing with the three long hairs that sprouted from a wart on his left cheek. Now he asked in a low voice:

'What is wrong with this store-room, Your Honour?'

Judge Dee told him about the weird scene he had witnessed when looking out of the window in the guest building opposite. 'The Prior remarked,' he concluded, 'that there is no window in the wall of this store-room facing the building where our quarters are, and apparently he was right. Yet I could hardly have dreamt it all! The naked woman must have lost her left arm some time ago, for I didn't notice any blood. If I had, I would have rushed to her at once to investigate, of course.'

'Well,' Tao Gan said, 'it shouldn't be too difficult to find a one-armed woman, there can't be many of them running about in this monastery. Could you see something of the furnishing of the room, sir?'

'No. I told you I got only one brief glimpse, didn't I?' Judge Dee said crossly.

'In any case it must have happened here in this store-room,' Tao Gan remarked cheerfully. 'I'll examine the wall, perhaps there's a window concealed behind all those spears and banners there. Perhaps even a trick window.'

Judge Dee followed his assistant's movements as he busied himself about the arms-rack. Tao Gan pulled the dusty silk banners aside, looked among the shafts of the spears and tridents and occasionally rapped the wall with his hard knuckles. He went about it quickly and efficiently, for this work belonged to his former trade. Tao Gan had originally been an itinerant swindler. One year before, shortly after the judge had taken up his post as magistrate of Han-yuan, he had extricated Tao Gan from a nasty situation, and then the wily trickster had mended his ways and entered Judge Dee's service. His wide knowledge of the ways of the underworld, and his skill in locating secret passages and forcing complicated locks, had proved very useful in the tracking down of elusive criminals, and helped the judge to solve more than one difficult case.

Leaving Tao Gan at his work, Judge Dee walked along the left wall, picking his way among the bags and boxes piled on the floor. He looked with distaste at the grotesque masks that were ogling him from the wall. He muttered, half to himself, half to Tao Gan:

'A weird creed, Taoism! Why should one need all that mummery of mystery plays and pompous religious ceremonies when we have the wise and crystal-clear teachings of our Master Confucius to guide us? One can only say for Taoism that it is at least a purely Chinese creed, and not an importation from the barbarous West, like Buddhism!'

'I gather that the Taoists had to institute monasteries and all that in order to be able to compete with the Buddhist crowd,' Tao Gan remarked.

'Bah!' the judge said angrily. His head was aching; the clammy atmosphere of the room penetrated even his padded robe.

'Look at this, sir!' Tao Gan suddenly exclaimed.

The judge quickly joined him. Tao Gan had pulled aside a gaudy silk banner that hung against the wall, near the large antique cupboard in the farthest corner. Under the dusty plaster that covered the brick wall one could still distinguish the outline of a window.

Silently the two men stared at the wall. Then Tao Gan looked uncomfortably at Judge Dee's impassive face. He said slowly:

Judge Dee and Tao Gan in the Store-room

19

'There was indeed a window here, but it must have been walled up a long time ago.'

Judge Dee looked up with a start. He said in a toneless voice:

'It is near the corner of the building. That means that it's about opposite the window through which I looked out.'

Tao Gan knocked on the wall. There was no doubt that it was solid. He took out his knife and, with its point, pried loose a piece of the plaster that covered the bricks with which the window had been blocked. He probed into the grooves among the bricks and along the outline of the window. He shook his head perplexedly. After some hesitation he said, diffidently:

'This monastery is very old, Your Honour. I have often heard people say that mysterious, inexplicable things will sometimes happen in such places. Scenes of times long gone by are seen again, and . . .' His voice trailed off.

The judge passed his hand over his eyes. He said pensively:

'The man I saw wore indeed a helmet of a type that is obsolete now, it was used by our soldiers more than a hundred years ago . . . This is strange, Tao Gan, very strange.' He thought for a long while, staring at the brick wall. Suddenly he looked hard at Tao Gan and said: 'I think I noticed a suit of armour of that same antiquated type among the stage costumes hanging on the wall. Yes, there it is!'

He walked up to a mail coat, with iron breastplates moulded like crouching dragons, that was hanging under the row of leering devils' masks. A pair of iron gloves and the empty scabbard of a long sword hung by its side.

'The round, close-fitting helmet belonging to that outfit is missing,' Judge Dee went on.

'Many of those costumes are incomplete, sir. Just odd pieces.'

The judge hadn't heard him. He continued:

'I couldn't see what the man was wearing on his body. I had the impression it was something dark. He had a broad back, and he was quite tall, I think.' He looked at Tao Gan with startled eyes. 'Almighty Heaven, Tao Gan, am I seeing ghosts?'

'I'll go and measure the depth of the window niches,' Tao Gan said.

While he was gone Judge Dee pulled his robe closer to his body; he felt shivery. He took a silk handkerchief from his sleeve and wiped his watering eyes. He reflected that he probably had a fever. Could it have been a hallucination?

Tao Gan came back.

'Yes,' he said, 'the wall is quite thick, nearly four feet, but still not thick enough for a secret room where a man can play about with a naked woman!'

'No, it isn't!' Judge Dee said dryly.

He turned to the old cupboard. The black-lacquered double doors were decorated with the design of a pair of dragons, facing each other and surrounded by a pattern of stylized flames. He pulled the doors open. The cupboard was empty but for a pile of folded monks' cowls. The design of the two dragons was repeated on the back wall. 'A fine antique specimen,' he remarked to Tao Gan, then added with a sigh: 'Well, I think that for the time being we'd better forget about the scene I saw, or thought I saw, and keep to the problems in hand. Three girls died here in this monastery, and that happened during the past year, mind you, not a hundred years ago! You'll remember that the one called Liu was said to have died from illness; Miss Huang committed suicide, and Miss Gao had a fatal accident – they said. I'll utilize this opportunity for asking the Abbot for some more information about those three cases. Let's go down!'

When they stepped out into the corridor they found the novice standing stock-still close to the door, peering ahead of him and listening intently. Seeing his pale face, the judge asked, astonished:

'What are you doing?'

'I . . . I thought I saw someone looking round the corner over there,' the novice stammered.

'Well,' Judge Dee said testily, 'you said yourself that people are coming and going here all the time, didn't you?'

'It was a soldier!' the boy muttered.

'A soldier?'

The novice nodded. He listened again, then said in a low voice:

'A hundred years ago there were many soldiers here. Rebels had occupied this monastery and fortified themselves here, together with their families.

The army took it, and slaughtered all of them, men, women and children.' He looked at the judge, his eyes wide with fear. 'They say that on stormy nights like this their ghosts walk here and act over again all those horrible scenes . . . Can't you hear anything, sir?'

Judge Dee listened.

'Only the rain!' he said impatiently. 'Take us downstairs, there's a draught here!'

4

The novice led them through a maze of passages
down to the ground floor of the east wing. Downstairs was a spacious corridor, lined by high
red-lacquered pillars, decorated with intricate
gilded wood-carving. It represented the design of
dragons sporting among clouds. The floor-boards
had been polished to a beautiful dark shine by the
felt shoes of the countless feet that had passed
there during past generations. When they arrived
in front of the assembly hall, Judge Dee said to
Tao Gan:

'While I am talking with the Abbot, you go to
the Prior and tell him about that broken axle. I
hope they can mend and replace it tonight.' Then
he added in a whisper: 'Try to get from the Prior
or someone else a good floor-plan of this dismal
place!'

The reception room was located near the
entrance of the main hall. When the novice
showed the judge in, he noticed with satisfaction
that the room was well heated by a brazier heaped
with glowing coals. Costly brocade wall-hangings
kept the warmth inside.

A tall, thin man rose from the gilded couch in
the back of the room and advanced across the
thick carpet to meet the judge. He was a stately

figure, looking taller still because of his long flow-
ing robe of yellow brocade and the high yellow
tiara, decorated with red tassels that hung down
his back. As he bade him welcome, the judge
noticed that the Abbot had curious, slate-coloured
eyes that seemed as immobile as his long, austere
face, smooth but for a thin moustache and a short,
wispy beard.

They sat down in high-backed armchairs by the
side of the couch. The novice prepared tea on
the red-lacquered table in the corner.

'I feel embarrassed,' Judge Dee began, 'that my
visit coincides with the big commemoration festival here. You'll have many guests staying in the
monastery; I greatly fear that my staying here
overnight will inconvenience you.'

The Abbot fixed him with his still eyes.
Although their gaze was directed at him, Judge
Dee had the weird impression that in fact it was
turned inward. The Abbot raised his long, curved
eye-brows. He replied in a low, dry voice:

'Your Honour's visit doesn't inconvenience us
in the least. The east wing of our poor monastery
has, on the second and third floor, more than forty
guest rooms – though none of those is of course
good enough for accommodating such a distinguished guest as our magistrate!'

'My quarters are most comfortable!' the judge
assured him hastily. He accepted the cup of hot
tea which the novice offered him respectfully with
both hands. He had a throbbing headache now
and found it difficult to formulate the usual polite

inquiries. He decided to come directly to the point, and said: 'I would have given myself the pleasure of visiting this famous monastery soon after I had taken up my duties in Han-yuan. However, pressing official business prevented me from leaving Han-yuan all through the past summer. In addition to benefiting by your instruction and admiring this interesting ancient building, I had planned also to ask you for some information.'

'I am entirely at Your Honour's service. What information might be required?'

'I would like to have a few more details about three deaths that occurred here last year,' the judge said. 'Just to complete my files, you see!'

The Abbot gave the novice a sign to leave. When the door had closed behind the youngster, the Abbot said with a deprecating smile:

'We have more than a hundred monks living here, Your Honour, not to speak of the lay brothers, novices, and occasional guests. Human life being submitted to the limitations set by Heaven, people fall ill and die, here as everywhere else. What particular deaths might Your Honour be referring to?'

'Well,' Judge Dee replied, 'going over the files in my tribunal I found, among the copies of death certificates forwarded to Han-yuan by this monastery, no less than three that referred to girls from outside. I gather that they had come to stay here to be initiated as nuns.' As he saw the Abbot knitting his thin eye-brows, he added with a quick smile: 'I don't recollect their names and other particulars. I would have looked them up before coming here, but, since my present visit was quite accidental . . .' He did not finish the sentence, looking expectantly at his host.

The Abbot nodded slowly.

'I think I know what cases Your Honour has in mind. Yes, there was a young lady from the capital, a Miss Liu who fell ill here last year. The learned Master Sun personally treated her, but . . .'

He suddenly broke off and looked fixedly at the door. Judge Dee turned round in his chair to see who had come in, but he only saw the door close again.

'Those insolent actors!' the Abbot exclaimed angrily. 'They come barging inside without even bothering to knock!' Noticing Judge Dee's astonished look, he quickly resumed: 'As usual we have hired a small troupe of professional actors, to assist the monks with the staging of the mystery plays that are performed on our commemoration day. They also play interludes, mainly acrobatics and juggling, and provide other light entertainment. They are quite useful, but they know of course nothing of monastic rules and behaviour.' He angrily stamped his staff on the floor and concluded: 'Next time we'll dispense with their services!'

'Yes,' Judge Dee said, 'I remember now that one girl of the surname Liu died of a lingering disease. May I ask you, just to get my record straight, who performed the autopsy?'

'Our Prior, Your Honour. He is a qualified physician.'

'I see. Wasn't there another girl who committed suicide?'

'That was a sad case!' the Abbot replied with a sigh. 'Quite an intelligent girl, but the very excitable type, you know; she suffered from hallucinations. I shouldn't have admitted her to begin with, but since she was so eager and since her parents insisted ... One night Miss Huang had been very nervous, and she took poison. The body was returned to the family, and she was buried in her native place.'

'And the third? I seem to remember that that was also a suicide, wasn't it?'

'No, it was an unfortunate accident, sir. Miss Gao was also a talented girl, deeply interested in the history of this monastery. She was always exploring the temple and adjacent buildings. Once the balustrade on the top floor of the south-east tower gave way when she was leaning over it, and she fell down into the ravine that borders our monastery on the east side.'

'There was no autopsy report attached to Miss Gao's documents,' the judge remarked.

The Abbot sadly shook his head.

'No, Your Honour,' he said slowly, 'the remains could not be recovered. At the bottom of the ravine there is a cleft over a hundred feet deep. Nobody has ever succeeded in exploring it.'

There was a pause. Then Judge Dee asked:

'Is the tower she fell from the one built on top

of the storeroom? In that case it's right opposite the east wing, where my quarters are.'

'Indeed.' The Abbot took a sip from his tea. Evidently he thought that it was time to conclude the interview. But Judge Dee made no move to take his leave. He caressed his long sidewhiskers for a while, then asked:

'You don't have nuns staying permanently here, do you?'

'No, fortunately not!' the Abbot answered with a thin smile. 'My responsibilities are sufficiently heavy without that! But, since this place, quite undeservedly of course, enjoys a high reputation in this province, many families which have daughters desirous of entering religion insist that they be initiated here. They receive instruction for a few weeks, and, when the nun's certificates have been bestowed upon them, they leave and settle in one of the nunneries elsewhere in our province.'

Judge Dee sneezed. When he had wiped his moustache with his silk handkerchief he said affably:

'Many thanks for your explanations! You'll understand, of course, that my questions were a mere formality. I never thought for one moment that there had been irregularities here.'

The Abbot nodded gravely. The judge emptied his teacup, then resumed:

'Just now you mentioned a Master Sun. Is that by any chance the famous scholar and writer Sun Ming, who a few years ago served in the Palace as Tutor of His Imperial Majesty?'

29

'Yes indeed! The Master's presence greatly honours this monastery! As you know, His Excellency had a most distinguished career. He served many years as Prefect of the capital, and retired after his two wives had died. Then he was appointed Imperial Tutor. When he left the Palace, his three sons had grown up and entered official life, so he decided to devote his remaining years to his metaphysical researches, and chose this monastery as his abode. His Excellency has been staying here now for two years already.' He nodded slowly, then went on with evident satisfaction: 'The Master's presence is a signal honour indeed! And, far from keeping himself aloof, he takes a most gratifying interest in all that goes on here, and regularly attends our religious services. Thus His Excellency is completely conversant with all our problems, and never grudges us his valuable advice.'

Judge Dee reflected ruefully that he would have to pay a courtesy visit to this exalted personage. He asked:

'In what part of the monastery has the Master taken up his abode?'

'The west tower has been placed at his disposal. Your Honour will presently meet the Master in the assembly hall, as he is watching the performance there. Your Honour will also see there Mrs Pao, a pious widow from the capital. She arrived here a few days ago, together with her daughter, called White Rose, who wishes to enter religion. Then there is also a Mr Tsung Lee, a poet of note, who has been staying here for a few weeks already. Those are our only guests. A number of others cancelled their intended visits because of the inclement weather. There's also the theatrical troupe of Mr Kuan Lai – but of course Your Honour won't be interested in that lowly crowd.'

Judge Dee angrily blew his nose. It had always struck him as unjust that people in general considered the stage a dishonourable profession, and actors and actresses more or less outcasts. He had expected from the Abbot a more humane attitude. He said:

'In my opinion actors perform a useful task. They provide at low cost suitable amusement for the common people and thereby enliven their often drab lives. Moreover, the historical plays acquaint the people with our great national past. An advantage, by the way, which your mystery plays are lacking.'

The Abbot said stiffly:

'Our mystery plays bear an allegorical rather than a historical character. They are meant to promulgate the Truth, and can therefore in no way be compared to common theatricals.' To take the edge off his remark, he added with a smile: 'Yet I hope that Your Honour won't find them lacking entirely in historical interest. The masks and costumes used were made over a hundred years ago in this monastery, they are valuable antiques. Allow me to lead Your Honour to the hall now. The performance has been going on since noon today, and now they are at the last scenes.

Thereafter a simple meagre meal will be served in the refectory. I hope that Your Honour will graciously consent to take part in it.'

Judge Dee hardly enjoyed the prospect of sitting in on an official banquet, but, as the magistrate of the district where the monastery was located, he couldn't possibly refuse.

'I accept with the greatest pleasure!' he replied jovially. They rose and the Abbot led him to the door.

When they were outside the Abbot quickly looked up and down the semi-obscure corridor. He seemed relieved at seeing it completely deserted. He politely led the judge to a high double door.

5

Upon entering the enormous hall they were greeted by the deafening sounds of gongs, cymbals and some strident stringed instruments. They came from the orchestra of monks, seated on a small platform on the left. The age-blackened roof of the hall was supported by a number of high thick pillars, among which were sitting over a hundred monks. The light of dozens of large paper lampions shone on their yellow robes.

The monks rose respectfully as the Abbot led Judge Dee along the open path in the middle to a raised platform by the side of the stage in the back of the hall. The Abbot sat down in a high-backed armchair of carved ebony, and bade the judge to be seated on his right. The third chair, on the Abbot's left, was unoccupied.

The small Prior came forward and reported that Master Sun had left but that he would be back soon. The Abbot nodded. He ordered him to bring fruit and other refreshments.

Judge Dee looked curiously at the magnificent pageant that was being enacted on the stage, which was lit by a row of red lampions. In the centre stood a high seat of gilded wood, on which was enthroned a handsome woman dressed in a red and green robe, glittering with gold ornaments. Her high chignon was decorated with a profusion of paper flowers, and she held a jade sceptre in her folded hands. Evidently she represented the Fairy Queen of the Taoist Western Paradise.

Eight figures, seven men and one woman, dressed in gorgeous long robes of embroidered silk, were executing a slow dance in front of the Queen, to the measure of the solemn music. They represented the Eight Immortals of the Taoist Pantheon, doing homage to their Queen.

'Are those two women nuns?' the judge asked.

'No,' the Abbot replied, 'the Queen is played by an actress of Kuan's troupe, Miss Ting is her name, I think. During the interval she did a rather good acrobatic dance, and juggled with cups and saucers. The Flower Fairy is Kuan's wife.'

Judge Dee watched the pageant for a while but found it rather boring. He reflected that perhaps he wasn't in the right mood for it. His head was throbbing and his hands and feet were ice-cold. He looked at the box over on the other side of the stage. It was enclosed on three sides by a lattice screen, so that the two women sitting inside could not be seen by the audience. One was a portly lady, rather heavily made up and wearing a beautiful dress of black damask, the other a young girl, also dressed in black, but not made up at all. She had a handsome, regular face, but her eyebrows were thicker than is thought becoming to a woman. Both were watching the performance in rapt attention. The Abbot, who had been following Judge Dee's gaze, said:

'That is Mrs Pao, and her daughter White Rose.'

The judge saw to his relief that the Eight Immortals were descending from the stage, followed by the Queen, who was led off by two novices dressed as pages. The music ended with a loud beat on the large bronze gong that reverberated through the hall. An appreciative murmur rose from the crowd of monks. Judge Dee sneezed again; he thought there was a nasty draught.

'A fine performance!' he remarked to the Abbot. Out of the corner of his eye he saw Tao Gan step up to the dais. He came to stand behind Judge Dee's chair and whispered:

'The Prior was busy, but I had a talk with the almoner, sir. He claims that they have no ground-plan of this place.'

Judge Dee nodded. The hall had become quiet again. A powerfully built man with a broad, mobile actor's face had appeared on the stage. Evidently he was Mr Kuan, the director of the troupe. He made a deep bow in the direction of the Abbot, then announced in a clear voice:

'By the leave of Your Holiness, we shall now, as usual, conclude the performance with a brief allegory. It represents the trials of the human soul seeking Salvation. The erring soul is played by Miss Ou-yang. She is harassed by Ignorance, played by a bear. Thank you!'

The astonished murmur from the audience was drowned in a mournful melody, interspersed with wailing blasts of the long brass trumpets that echoed through the hall. A slender girl dressed in a white robe with wide sleeves ascended the stage and started to execute a slow dance, turning round and round so that her sleeves and the trailing ends of her red sash fluttered about. Judge Dee looked intently at her heavily made-up face then tried to get a glimpse of the girl in the box on the other side of the stage. But the portly lady was leaning forward, so that he couldn't see her daughter. Astonished, he said to Tao Gan:

'That isn't an actress, that is Miss Pao, the girl who was sitting over in that screened box there!'

Tao Gan raised himself on tiptoe. He said:

'A young girl is still sitting there, Your Honour. Next to a rather fat lady.'

Craning his neck Judge Dee had another look at the box.

'Yes, so she is,' he said slowly. 'But she is looking as scared as if she had seen a ghost. I wonder why that actress has made herself up so as to resemble Miss Pao. Perhaps she . . .'

He suddenly broke off. A big man dressed as an awe-inspiring warrior had appeared on the stage. His tight-fitting black costume accentuated his lithe, muscular body. The red light shone on the round helmet on his head and the long sword that he whirled round. His face was painted red, with long white streaks across his cheeks.

'That's the man I saw with the naked girl!' Judge Dee whispered at Tao Gan. 'Call the director here!'

The warrior was a superb swordsman. While

dancing round the girl he made several quick passes at her with the long sword. She evaded the thrusts gracefully. Then he moved closer to her, stepping deftly to the measure of the drums. His sword swung close over her head, then came down in a wicked stroke that missed her shoulder by a hairbreadth. A sharp cry came from ladies' box. Judge Dee saw that Miss Pao had risen and was gazing with horror-stricken face at the two figures on the stage, her hands gripping the balustrade. The portly lady spoke to her, but she didn't seem to hear.

The judge looked at the stage again.

'One wrong move and we'll have an accident!' he said worriedly to the Abbot. 'Who is that fellow, anyway?'

'He is an actor called Mo Mo-te,' the Abbot replied. 'I agree that he comes far too close. But he's being more careful now.'

The warrior had indeed stopped his attacks on the girl; he was now executing a series of complicated feints some distance from her. His painted face flashed weirdly in the light of the lampions.

Tao Gan appeared by the side of Judge Dee's chair, and presented Mr Kuan Lai, the director of the troupe.

'Why didn't you announce that Mo Mo-te would take part in the allegory?' the judge asked sharply.

Kuan smiled.

'We often improvise a bit, sir,' he said. 'Mo Mo-te likes to show off his skill as a swordsman,

therefore he assumed the role of Doubt, torment-
ing the erring soul.'

'It comes too close to real torment for my taste,'
Judge Dee said curtly. 'Look, he is attacking the
dancer again!'

Now the girl evidently had difficulty in evading
the vicious sword-thrusts the warrior was aiming
at her; her breast was heaving and sweat streaked
her made-up face. The judge thought there was
something wrong with her left arm. He couldn't
see it clearly because of the wide, swirling sleeve,
but she seemed unable to use it, keeping it close
to her body all the time. He said angrily to himself
that, if he was starting to see one-armed girls
everywhere, he would have to take hold of himself. He sat up. A quick swordstroke cut off a
corner from the dancer's fluttering left sleeve. A
frightened cry sounded from the ladies' box.

The judge got up to shout to the warrior to stop.
But at the same time the girl whistled, and now a
huge black bear came ambling on to the stage. He
turned his large head to the warrior, who quickly
retreated to a corner of the stage. Judge Dee sat
down again.

The bear growled, then slowly went up to the
girl, shaking its heavy head. The girl seemed in
great fear, she covered her face with her right
sleeve. The bear kept on advancing. The music
had ceased, all was deadly quiet.

'The ugly brute will kill her!' the judge said
angrily.

'It belongs to Miss Ou-yang, Your Honour,'

Kuan said reassuringly. 'The chain on his collar is attached to that pillar at the back of the stage.'

Judge Dee said nothing. He didn't like this at all. He noticed that Miss Pao had resumed her seat, she seemed to have lost interest in the show. But her face was still very pale.

The warrior made a few final feints with his sword, then disappeared. The bear was walking slowly round the girl, who was now executing a quick dance, gyrating on the tips of her toes.

'Where is that fellow off to?' Judge Dee asked Kuan.

'He'll be going to our dressing-room, sir,' the director answered. 'He'll be anxious to get rid of his make-up and his costume.'

'Was he on the stage about one hour ago?' the judge asked again.

'He has been on ever since the interval,' Kuan replied with a smile. 'And he had to wear a heavy wooden mask all through. He was acting the part of the Spirit of Death, you know. Anyone else would have been tired out now, but he is an extra-ordinarily strong fellow. Just now he came on again because he couldn't resist the temptation to show off his skill.'

Judge Dee hadn't heard his last words. His eyes were riveted on the stage, where the bear had now raised itself on its haunches. It was groping with its enormous paws for the girl, growling angrily. The girl drew back, but suddenly the bear was on her with amazing swiftness. The girl fell on the

A Poet Taunts a Taoist Abbot

floor, and the animal stood over her, opening its huge jaws lined with long yellow teeth.

The judge suppressed a cry. Suddenly the girl crept out from under the hulking animal and came gracefully to her feet. She patted the bear on its head, then took it by its collar and made a deep bow. She led the animal off-stage amid thunderous applause from the audience.

Judge Dee wiped the perspiration from his brow. In the excitement he had forgotten all about his cold, but now he realized again that he had a bad headache. He wanted to get up, but the Abbot laid his hand on his arm and said:

'Now Mr Tsung Lee, the poet, will pronounce the epilogue!'

A young man with a shrewd, beardless face stood in the centre of the empty stage. He made a bow, then began in a sonorous, well-modulated voice:

'All you good men and women! Noble Excellencies!
Monks and lay brothers, and all you novices!
To all of you who kindly watched our humble play
Of the stirring story of that poor erring soul
Losing her struggle with Doubt and Ignorance, I say:
Never despair of reaching in the end your goal!
However long the forces of Darkness scheme,
The Truth of Tao shall all of you redeem.

Hear now the Sublime Truth, expressed in clumsy
verse:
All wicked evil, Truth and Reason shall disperse,
Defeat for ever the deadly shades of night,
Dissolve the morning clouds in the Eternal Light!'

He made another deep bow and left the stage.
The orchestra struck up the finale.

Judge Dee looked questioningly at the Abbot.
Spoken in a monastery called Morning Cloud, the
last line about 'dissolving morning clouds' was
most inauspicious, even rude. The Abbot barked
at the director:

'Get me that poet here!' And, to the judge: 'The
impudent rascal!'

When the young man was standing in front of
them, the Abbot addressed him harshly:

'What made you add that last line, Mr Tsung?
It completely spoilt the auspicious atmosphere of
this solemn occasion!'

The young man seemed quite at ease. He gave
the Abbot a quizzical look and replied with a
smile:

'The last line, Your Holiness? I had feared that
the line before last might perhaps be considered
inappropriate. It's not always easy to find the right
rhymes on the spot, you know!'

The Abbot was about to make an angry retort,
but Tsung continued placidly:

'Short verses are easier, of course. Like this one,
for instance:

One abbot up in the hall,
One abbot under the floor
In all two abbots –
One preaches to the monks,
The other to the maggots.'

The Abbot angrily stamped his staff on the floor. His face was twitching. Judge Dee expected him to burst out in a fit of rage. But he succeeded in mastering himself. He said coldly:

'You may go, Mr Tsung.'

He rose. The judge noticed that his hands were trembling. Judge Dee took leave of him with a few polite phrases.

As they were walking towards the exit, the judge said to Tao Gan:

'We'll go now to the actors' dressing-room, I must have a talk with that fellow Mo Mo-te. Do you know where it is?'

'Yes, Your Honour, on the same floor as mine, in a side corridor.'

'I never saw such a rabbit-warren!' Judge Dee muttered. 'And what is all that nonsense about no ground-plan being available? They are required by law to have one!'

'The almoner claims, sir, that the section higher up, that is, the part of the monastery beyond the temple, is closed to everybody except the Abbot and the ordained monks. That forbidden part may not be charted or depicted. The almoner agreed that it was awkward not to have a plan, for this is a very large place. Even the monks themselves sometimes lose their way.'

'A preposterous situation!' the judge said peevishly. 'Just because the Palace has deigned to show interest in the Taoist creed, those people think they are above the law! And I hear that Buddhist influence is also growing at Court. I don't know which of the two is worse!'

He walked over to the office on the opposite side of the hall. He told the monk in charge there that after he had changed he wanted a novice to take him to Master Sun's quarters. Tao Gan borrowed a lantern from the monk, then they waited a while in front of the office to let the throng of monks who were leaving the hall file past them.

'Look at all those able-bodied-fellows!' Judge Dee said sourly. 'They ought to do their duty to society, marry and raise children!'

He sneezed.

Tao Gan gave him a worried look. He had come to know the judge as a man of a remarkably equable temper, even if he was annoyed he rarely showed it so clearly. He asked:

'Did that solemn Abbot give a satisfactory explanation of those three deaths that occurred here?'

'He did not!' the judge said emphatically. 'It is just as I thought, there are highly suspicious features. When we are back in Han-yuan, I shall first obtain from the families of the dead girls more details about their background, then we'll come back to this monastery with Sergeant Hoong, Ma Joong, Chiao Tai, the scribes and a dozen constables, and institute a thorough investigation. And I'll not announce that visit beforehand, mind you! That's the little surprise I have in store for our friend the Abbot!'

6

Tao Gan nodded contentedly. Then he said:

'The almoner told me the same story about the ghosts of the people who were killed here a hundred years ago. I now know why that novice was listening so keenly up there in the corridor!'

'Why?' Judge Dee asked, wiping his moustache.

'It is, sir, said that those ghostly apparitions sometimes whisper one's name. That means that the person who hears them will die soon.'

'Silly superstitions! Let's go upstairs to the dressing-room of those actors.'

When they had arrived on the first landing, Judge Dee looked casually into the narrow, semi-dark corridor on their right. He halted. A slender girl in a white dress was hurrying along away from them.

'That's the girl with the bear!' the judge said quickly to Tao Gan. 'I want to talk to her! What's her name again?'

'Miss Ou-yang, sir.'

The judge went after the white figure. When he was close behind her he said:

'Wait a moment, Miss Ou-yang!'

She swung round with a frightened cry. The judge saw that her face was of a deadly pallor and her eyes wide with fear. It struck him again that she closely resembled Miss Pao. He said kindly:

'You needn't be afraid, Miss Ou-yang. I only wanted to congratulate you on your performance. I must say that – '

'Thank you, sir!' the girl interrupted in a soft, cultured voice. 'I must hurry along now, I must . . .'

She looked anxiously past the judge and made to turn round again.

'Don't run away!' Judge Dee ordered curtly. 'I am the magistrate, and I want to talk with you. You seem quite upset. Is that actor Mo Mo-te perhaps bothering you?'

She impatiently shook her small head.

'I must go and feed my bear,' she said quickly.

The judge saw that all the time she kept her left arm close to her body. He asked sharply:

'What is wrong with your left arm? Did Mo wound you with his sword?'

'Oh no, a long time ago my bear scratched me there. Now I must really – '

'I fear that Your Honour didn't like my poetry,' a cheerful voice spoke up behind them. Judge Dee turned round. He saw Tsung Lee, who was making an exaggerated bow.

'I did not, young man!' the judge said, annoyed. 'If I had been the Abbot I would have had you thrown out then and there!'

He turned to the girl again. But she had disappeared.

'The Abbot'll think twice before he has me

47

thrown out, sir!' the young poet said smugly. 'My late father, Dr Tsung, was a patron of this monastery, and my family still regularly donates substantial sums to it.'

Judge Dee looked him up and down.

'So you are a son of the retired Governor Tsung Fa-men,' he said. 'The Governor was a great scholar, I have read his hand-book on provincial administration. He wouldn't have liked your clumsy doggerels!'

'I only wanted to rile the Abbot a bit,' Tsung said with an embarrassed air. 'The fellow is such a self-important stick! My father didn't think much of him, sir.'

'Even so,' the judge said, 'your poem was in extremely bad taste. And what on earth did you mean by that silly rhyme about two abbots?'

'Doesn't Your Honour know?' Tsung Lee asked astonished. 'Two years ago Jade Mirror, the former Abbot of this monastery died – or was "translated", as the correct term is, I think. He was embalmed, and now sits enthroned in the crypt under the Founder's shrine, in the sanctum. Jade Mirror was a very holy man – both dead and alive.'

Judge Dee made no comment. He had worries enough without going into the life histories of the abbots of the Morning Cloud Monastery. He said:

'I am on my way to the actors' dressing-room, so I won't detain you here further.'

'I was going there too, sir,' the young man said respectfully. 'May I show Your Honour the way?'

He took them round the corner into a long corridor lined by doors on both sides.

'Is Miss Ou-yang's room near here?' the judge asked.

'Somewhat farther along,' Tsung replied. 'But I wouldn't go there without her, Your Honour! That bear is dangerous.'

'She must be in her room,' Judge Dee said. 'Didn't you see her when you came up to us, just now?'

'Of course I didn't see her!' the poet said, astonished. 'How could she have been here? Just before coming up I had a talk with her, down in the hall. She's still there!'

The judge gave him a sharp look, then glanced at Tao Gan. His assistant shook his head, a perplexed expression on his long face.

Tsung Lee knocked on a door near the end of the corridor. They entered a large, untidy room. Kuan Lai and two women quickly rose from the round table where they were sitting and greeted the judge with low bows.

Kuan presented the nice-looking young girl as Miss Ting, the actress who had acted the part of the Queen of the Western Paradise. He added that her specialities were acrobatic dancing and juggling. The dowdy middle-aged woman he presented as his wife.

Judge Dee said a few kind words about the performance. The director seemed overwhelmed by the interest shown in his troupe by this distinguished person. He didn't quite know whether he ought to ask the judge to sit down with them, or whether that would be too presumptuous. Judge Dee solved his quandary by sitting down uninvited. Tsung Lee took the seat opposite, where a wine-jug of coarse earthenware was standing. Tao Gan took up his position behind Judge Dee's chair. Then the judge asked:

'Where are Miss Ou-yang and Mo Mo-te? I would like to offer them my compliments too. Mo is a fine swordsman, and Miss Ou-yang's performance with the bear made my hair stand on end!'

This kind address apparently failed to put the director at his ease. His hand trembled when he poured out a cup of wine for the judge so that he spilt some of it on the table. He sat down awkwardly and said:

'Mo Mo-te will have gone to the store-room to return his costume, sir.' Pointing at the pile of crumpled, red-stained sheets of paper on the dressing-table, he added: 'Apparently he has been in here already to remove the paint from his face. As to Miss Ou-yang, she told me downstairs that she would come here after she had fed her bear.'

Judge Dee got up, and walked over to the dressing-table, pretending that he wanted to adjust his cap in front of the mirror there. He looked casually at the crumpled sheets of paper and the pots with ointments and paint. He reflected that the red stains on the paper might as well be blood. When he was resuming his seat, he noticed that Mrs Kuan was looking apprehensively at him. He took a sip of his wine, and asked Kuan about the stage technique of historical plays.

The director set out on a long explanation. The judge only half listened; he was trying to follow at the same time the conversation the others had struck up.

'Why didn't you go to help Miss Ou-yang to feed the bear?' Tsung Lee asked Miss Ting. 'She'd have liked that, I am sure!'

'Mind your own business!' Miss Ting said curtly. 'Keep to your roses, will you?'

Tsung Lee said with a sly grin:

'Well, Miss Pao is rather an attractive girl, so why shouldn't I make poems for her? I even made one for you, dear. Here it is:

> True love, false love,
> Love of tomorrow, of yesterday –
> Plus and minus
> Keep us gay,
> Minus and minus,
> Heaven'll fine us!'

Judge Dee looked round. Miss Ting's face had grown scarlet. He heard Mrs Kuan say:

'You'd better mind your language, Mr Tsung!'

'I only wanted to warn her,' Tsung Lee said unperturbed. 'Don't you know that popular song they are now singing in the capital?' He hummed a fetching tune, beating the measure with his forefinger, then sung the words in a low, pleasant voice:

51

'Two times ten and still unwed,
There's yet hope for a bright tomorrow.
Three times eight and alone in bed,
There's nothing ahead but cold and sorrow!'

Miss Ting wanted to make an angry remark, but now Judge Dee intervened. He addressed the poet coldly:

'You interrupt my conversation, Mr Tsung. I must also inform you that I have but a feeble sense of humour. Reserve your witticisms for a more appreciative audience.' And, to Kuan: 'I have to go up and change for the banquet. Don't bother to see me out!'

Motioning Tao Gan to follow him he went out, closing the door in the face of the disconcerted director. He said to his lieutenant:

'Before I go up I'll try to find Mo Mo-te. You stay here and drink a few more rounds with those people. I perceive all kinds of undercurrents. You must try to find out what's going on. By the way, what did that paltry poet mean with his plus and minus?'

Tao Gan looked embarrassed. He cleared his throat, then replied:

'They are coarse terms used in the street, Your Honour. Plus means man and minus woman.'

'I see. Well, when Miss Ou-yang turns up, try to verify how long she was downstairs. She can't have been in two places at the same time!'

'That poet may have lied about meeting her in the hall, sir! And again when he pretended that he hadn't seen her talking to us. It's true that the corridor is very narrow, and that we were standing in between, but he could hardly have missed seeing her!'

'If Tsung Lee spoke the truth,' the judge remarked, 'the girl we talked to in the corridor must have been Miss Pao, posing as Miss Ou-yang. But no, that's wrong! The girl we met kept her arm close to her body and Miss Pao used both her arms when she gripped the balustrade, frightened by Mo's sword-play on the stage. I can't make head or tail of it! Find out what you can, then come up to my room!'

He took the lantern over from Tao Gan, and went to the stairs. Tao Gan went back into the actors' room.

Judge Dee thought he remembered the way to the store-room well enough. While climbing the staircase in the next building he noticed that his back and legs were aching. He wondered whether that was due to his cold or to the unaccustomed going up and down stairs all the time. He thought he rather liked Kuan, but Tsung Lee was the type of fresh youngster he had small use for. The poet seemed to be on very friendly terms with the actors. Apparently he was interested in Miss Pao, but, since she was about to become a nun, there seemed to be little hope for the poet there. His indelicate doggerel about Miss Ting suggested a relation between her and Miss Ou-yang. But the morals of those people were no concern of his, it was Mo Mo-te who interested him.

He heaved a sigh when at last he found himself on the draughty landing on the floor above the temple nave. Through the lattice-work he heard the monotonous chant of the monks coming up from the well, apparently practising vespers.

Upon entering the corridor on his right he was astonished to see that there was no light. But when he held his lantern high, he realized that he had taken the wrong passage. There were no windows on the wall on his right, and this passage was narrower than the one leading to the store-room. Cobwebs hung from the low rafters. He was about to turn round and retrace his steps when he suddenly heard a murmur of voices.

He stood still and listened, wondering where these whispers might be coming from. The corridor was deserted, and at the end there was a heavy iron grille. He walked up to the entrance, but there the vague whispers were drowned by the chant of the monks. With a puzzled frown he walked back to the middle of the passage, looking for a door.

Here he heard the whispering again, but he couldn't make out one word of what was being said. Suddenly he caught his own name: Dee Jendjieh.

Then everything was silent.

7

The judge tugged angrily at his beard. The ghostly voice had disturbed him more than he cared to admit. Then he took hold of himself. Probably some monks were talking about him in another room or passage near there. Often the echo played queer tricks in such old buildings. He stood listening for a while, but did not hear anything. The whispers had ceased.

Shrugging his shoulders, he walked back to the landing. He now saw that he had indeed taken a wrong turn. The passage leading to the store-room was on the other side. He quickly walked round the well and now found the right corridor; he recognized the three narrow windows on his right. The door of the store-room was standing ajar. He heard voices coming from inside.

As he went in he saw to his disappointment that there were only two monks. They were busy with the lock of a large box of red-lacquered leather. He didn't see Mo Mo-te, but a quick glance at the wall on the left showed that the round iron helmet was now hanging in its place above the coat of mail, and that the long sword had been put back in the scabbard. He asked the elder man:

'Have you seen the actor Mo Mo-te?'

'No, Your Honour,' the monk answered. 'But we have only just come in, we must have missed him.'

The man spoke politely enough, but the judge didn't like the surly look of the younger monk, a tall, broad-shouldered fellow who stared at him suspiciously.

'I wanted to compliment him on his skill in sword-fighting,' Judge Dee said casually. Apparently the actor had returned to Kuan's room, and there Tao Gan would keep an eye on him.

He set out on the long way to his own quarters on the third floor of the east wing.

He felt very tired when at last he knocked on the door of the dressing-room. One of the maids opened the door. The others were preparing the rice for the evening meal on the brazier in the corner.

In the bedroom Judge Dee found his three wives gathered round the tea-table, engaged in a game of dominoes. As they rose to greet him, his First Lady said with satisfaction:

'You are just in time for a game, before we start dinner.'

The judge looked wistfully at the pieces on the table, for dominoes was his favourite game. He said:

'Much to my regret I can't have dinner with you here. I have to take part in the banquet the Abbot is giving downstairs. There's a former Imperial Tutor staying here too, I couldn't possibly refuse.'

'Good Heavens!' his First Lady exclaimed, 'that means that I must pay a courtesy visit to his wife!'

'No, the Tutor is a widower. But I'll have to call on him before the banquet. Take my ceremonial robes out, will you?'

He blew his nose vigorously.

'I am glad that I won't have to get dressed!' she said with relief. 'But it's a shame that you should be up and about. You certainly have a head-cold. Look, your eyes are watering!'

While she opened the clothes box and started to lay out Judge Dee's green brocade robe, his third wife said:

'I'll make you a poultice of orange peel. If you keep that round your head, you'll feel much better tomorrow!'.

'How can I attend the banquet with a bandage round my head!' the judge exclaimed aghast. 'I'd look like a fool!'

'You can pull your cap down over it, can't you?' his First Lady said practically as she helped him change. 'Nobody'll notice it!'

The judge mumbled some protests, but his third wife had already taken a handful of dried orange rinds from their medicine chest and was putting them in a bowl of hot water. When they had been soaked well, his second wife wrapped them up in a linen bandage and together they wound it tightly round his head. His First Lady pulled his velvet cap well down and said:

'There you are, it doesn't show at all!'

Judge Dee thanked them. He promised that he would come up as soon as the banquet was over.

When he was at the door he turned round and added:

'All kinds of people are about here tonight, so you'd better keep the door to the corridor locked and barred, and let nobody in before the maids have ascertained who it is.'

He went into the dressing-room, where Tao Gan stood waiting for him. The judge told the maids to go to the bedroom to serve tea to his wives. He sat down with Tao Gan at the corner table and asked in a low voice:

'Did Mo Mo-te go to Kuan's room? I just missed him.'

'No,' Tao Gan replied, 'he must be walking about somewhere. But soon after you had left, Miss Ou-yang came in. Without make-up she doesn't resemble Miss Pao, although she has the same regular, oval face. I think it was Miss Pao we met in the corridor, for you'll remember that she spoke in a soft, pleasant voice, and Miss Ou-yang's is rather harsh and a bit hoarse. And although I don't claim to be a connoisseur of women, I think the girl we met was plumper than Miss Ou-yang, who is rather on the bony side.'

'Yet the girl we met didn't use her left arm, exactly like Miss Ou-yang. What did she talk about?'

'She is rather a taciturn girl, it seems. She only became a bit more lively when I made her join a conversation with Miss Ting about acrobatic dances. I referred casually to Tsung Lee having met Miss Ou-yang in the hall. She only remarked sourly that he was a bore. Then I said that you hadn't liked the abrupt way she disappeared in the midst of a talk with you. She gave me a sharp look, and said, vaguely, that her bear needed a lot of attention.'

'Somebody is fooling us!' Judge Dee exclaimed, angrily tugging at his beard. Then he asked: 'What did they say about Mo Mo-te?'

'It seems he is a man of rather erratic habits. He'll join the troupe for a month or so, then disappear again. He always acts the part of the villain, and Kuan maintains that it tends to make a man a bit touchy in the end. I gathered that Mo is rather fond of Miss Ting, but she won't have him. Therefore Mo is fearfully jealous of Miss Ou-yang; he suspects that the two girls are having a little affair of their own together, just as Tsung Lee suggested in his poem. Kuan agrees that Mo went a bit too far in frightening Miss Ou-yang with that sword-dance, but he added that with that nasty bear of hers about she needn't fear anybody. The animal follows its mistress about and obeys her like a lap-dog, but nobody else dares to come near the brute. It has a vicious temper.'

'It's a vexing puzzle!' the judge muttered. 'Suppose that Miss Ou-yang or Miss Pao was running away from Mo Mo-te when we met her in the corridor, and that he is a dangerous maniac. That would fit in with the weird scene I saw through the window. The man I saw must have been Mo Mo-te, but who was the girl he was assaulting? We must find out whether there are other women staying in this monastery besides the ones we know about.'

'I didn't dare to inquire about a mutilated woman without your orders, sir,' Tao Gan said. 'But I don't think that there are any other women staying here besides Mrs Kuan and the two actresses, and Mrs Pao with her daughter, of course.'

'Don't forget that we have seen only a very small part of this monastery,' the judge said. 'Heaven knows what goes on in the section forbidden to outsiders! And we don't even have a map of the place! Well, I'll go and call on Master Sun now. You go back to the actors. When the elusive Mo Mo-te turns up you stick to him like a leech and go to the banquet with him. I'll see you there later.'

In the corridor a novice stood waiting for the judge.

'Do we have to go outside to reach the west tower?' Judge Dee asked. The rain was still clattering against the shutters, he didn't like to get his ceremonial robe wet.

'Oh no, sir!' the novice replied. 'We'll go to the west wing by way of the passage over the temple hall.'

'More stairs!' the judge muttered.

8

They made the now familiar journey to the landing over the temple nave. The novice took the passage opposite the one that led to the store-room. It was a long, straight corridor, lit by only one broken lantern.

While walking behind the novice, Judge Dee suddenly had the uncomfortable feeling that someone was watching him from behind. He halted in his steps and looked over his shoulder. He saw something dark flit past the entrance at the far end of the passage. It could have been a man in a grey robe. As he walked on he asked the novice:

'Do the monks often use this passage too?'

'Oh no, sir! I only took it because it saves us from going outside in the rain. All people who have business in the west tower go up there by the spiral staircase, near the portal in front of the refectory.'

When they had arrived in the small square hall in the west side of the building, the judge stood still in order to orientate himself.

'Where does that lead to?' he asked, pointing at a narrow door on his right.

'It gives access to the Gallery of Horrors, sir, in the left wing of the central court, behind the temple. But we novices are not allowed to go in there.'

'I would have thought that viewing that gallery would be a good deterrent to committing sins!' Judge Dee remarked. He knew that every larger Taoist monastery had a gallery where the punishments meted out to sinners in the Ten Taoist Hells were painted in lurid detail on the wall, or plastically represented by statues moulded in clay or sculptured in wood.

As they ascended a few steps on their left, the novice warned:

'You'll have to be careful, sir! The balustrade of the landing in front of the Master's room is being repaired. Please keep close to me!'

When he was standing on the platform in front of a high, red-lacquered door Judge Dee saw that part of the balustrade was indeed missing. He looked down into the dark shaft of the staircase. It seemed very deep.

'These are the stairs I mentioned just now, they lead down to the west wing,' the novice explained. 'They come out in front of the refectory, three floors down.'

Judge Dee gave him his large red visiting-card. The novice knocked on the door.

A booming voice told them to come in.

In the brilliant light of four high silver candelabras a tall man sat reading at a huge desk, piled with books and papers. The novice bowed deeply and placed the visiting-card on the table. Master

Judge Dee Visits an Exalted Person

63

Sun glanced at it, then quickly got up and came forward to meet the judge.

'So you are the magistrate of our district!' he said in a deep, sonorous voice. 'Welcome to the Monastery of the Morning Cloud, Dee!'

Judge Dee bowed, his arms respectfully folded in his wide sleeves.

'This person had never dared to hope, sir,' he said, 'that a mishap on the road would provide the long-looked-for opportunity of paying my respects to such an eminent person.'

'Let's dispense with all empty formality, Dee!' Sun said jovially. 'Sit down here in front of my desk while I put these papers in order.' As he resumed his seat in the armchair behind his desk he said to the novice, who had poured out two cups of tea: 'Thank you, my boy, you may go now. I'll look after the guest myself.'

While sipping the fragrant jasmine tea, the judge looked at his host as he was quickly sorting out the papers before him. He was as tall as the judge but more heavily built. His thick neck was half buried in his broad, bulging shoulders. Judge Dee knew the Master must be nearly sixty, but his rosy, round face didn't show a single wrinkle. A short, grey ringbeard grew round his chin, his silvery grey hair was combed back straight from the broad forehead and plastered to his large, round head. Having assumed the status of Taoist recluse, the Master wore no cap. He wore his moustache trimmed short, but he had thick, tufted eyebrows.

Everything about him indicated that this was a remarkable personality.

Judge Dee read some of the scrolls inscribed with Taoist texts that covered the walls. Then Sun pushed the sorted-out papers away. Fixing the judge with his piercing eyes, he asked:

'You referred to a mishap on the road. Nothing serious, I hope?'

'Oh no, sir! I stayed for two weeks in the capital, and early this morning left there to go back to Han-yuan, in a tilt-cart. We had hoped to be home before the evening meal. But shortly after we had crossed the district frontier, the weather got worse, and when we were up in the mountains here, the axle broke. Therefore I had to ask for shelter in this monastery. We'll leave tomorrow morning. I am told these storms don't last long.'

'Bad luck for you, good luck for me!' Sun said with a smile. 'I always enjoy talking with capable young officials. You should have come here earlier, Dee! This monastery is within your jurisdiction.'

'I have been very remiss, sir!' the judge said hastily. 'The fact is that there was some trouble in Han-yuan and – '

'I heard all about it!' Sun interrupted him. 'You did good work there, Dee. Prevented a major disturbance of the peace, in fact.'

The judge acknowledged the compliment with a bow. He said:

'I shall certainly come back here soon, in order to be further instructed by Your Excellency.' Since this learned and experienced high official was apparently in a friendly mood, he thought he ought to try to settle at least one aspect of the problem of the mutilated naked woman. After a momentary hesitation he resumed: 'Might I take the liberty of consulting Your Excellency about a curious experience I had here just now?'

'By all means! What happened, and where?'

'As a matter of fact,' Judge Dee said, somewhat embarrassed, 'I don't know what happened exactly. When I went up to the quarters assigned to me, I saw for a brief moment a scene that must have happened more than a hundred years ago, when the soldiers slaughtered the rebels here. Are such things possible?'

Sun leaned back in his armchair. He said gravely:

'I wouldn't call it impossible, Dee. Doesn't it often happen that upon entering an empty room you definitely know that someone has been there a few moments before? You can't explain that, it's just a feeling. It means that the person who was there before you left something of himself behind. Yet he did nothing special there, perhaps he just looked at a book or wrote a letter. Now, suppose that the same man died a violent death in that room. It is only to be expected that the terrible emotion of that moment impregnates the atmosphere of that room, and so deeply too that it lingers on for years. If a hyper-sensitive person, or a person who has become hyper-sensitive because he is very tired, happens to enter there, he may well perceive that imprint. Don't you think

66

that some such reasoning might explain what you saw, Dee?'

The judge nodded slowly. Evidently Sun had given much thought to such abstruse matters. The explanation did not convince him, but it was a possibility he would have to keep in mind. He said politely:

'You are probably right, sir. I am indeed rather tired, and on top of that I caught a cold in the rain outside. In that condition – '

'A cold? I haven't had a cold for thirty years!' Sun cut him short. 'But I live according to a strict discipline, you know, nurturing my vital essence.'

'Do you believe in the Taoist theory about reaching immortality in this life, sir?' Judge Dee asked, somewhat disappointed.

'Of course not!' Sun replied disdainfully. 'Every man is immortal, but only in so far that he lives on in his offspring. Heaven has limited human life to a few score years, and all attempts at prolonging it beyond that limit by artificial means are futile. What we should strive after is to pass our limited life with a healthy mind and body. And that can be achieved by living in a more natural manner than we are wont to, especially by improving our diet. Be careful with your diet, Dee!'

'I am a follower of Confucius,' the judge said, 'but I fully admit that Taoism also contains deep wisdom.'

'Taoism continues where Confucius left off,' Master Sun remarked. 'Confucianism explains how man should behave as a member of an ordered society. Taoism explains man's relations to the Universe – of which that social order is but one aspect.'

Judge Dee was not exactly in the mood for an involved philosophical discussion. But he felt he should not take his leave before having tried to verify two points. After a suitable pause he asked:

'Could it be that undesirable elements from outside are roaming about here, sir? Just now, when the novice was taking me here, I had the feeling that we were being followed. While passing the corridor that links the nave with this tower, to be precise.'

Master Sun gave him a searching look. He thought for a while, then he asked suddenly:

'Are you fond of fish?'

'Yes, I am,' the judge replied, nonplussed.

'There you are! Fish clogs the system, my dear fellow. It makes the blood-circulation sluggish, and that affects the nerves. That's what makes you see and hear things that aren't there! Rhubarb is what you need, I think. It purifies the blood. I'll look it up, I have rather a fine collection of medical books. Remind me tomorrow morning. I'll draw up a detailed dieting schedule for you.'

'Thank you, sir. I hate to trouble you, but I would be most grateful for your elucidation on another point that has often puzzled me. I have heard people say that some Taoists, under the pretext of religious motives, practise orgies in secret, and force young women to take part in those. Is there any truth in these allegations?'

'Utter nonsense, of course!' Master Sun exclaimed. 'Heavens, Dee, how could we Taoists indulge in orgies, on our strict diet? Orgies, forsooth!' He rose and added: 'Now we had better go downstairs. The banquet is about to start and the Abbot'll be waiting for us. I must warn you that he's not a very profound scholar, but he means well, and he manages this monastery quite efficiently.'

'That must be an onerous task,' Judge Dee said as he rose also. 'The monastery is like a small city! I would like to explore it a bit, but I was told that there doesn't exist a floor-plan, and that anyway the part beyond the temple is closed to visitors.'

'All that hocus-pocus! Only meant to impress the credulous crowd! I have told the Abbot Heaven knows how many times that the monastery is required to have a floor-plan; article 28 of the Regulations of officially-recognized Places of Worship. Look here, Dee, I can orientate you in a trice.' Walking over to the side wall he pointed to a scroll hanging there and went on: 'This is a diagram I drew myself. It is really quite simple. The people who built this place two hundred years ago wanted the ground-plan to represent the universe, and at the same time Man, as a miniature replica of it. The outline of the whole complex is an oval, which represents the Original Beginning. It faces south, and is built on four levels against the mountain slope. All along the east side is a deep ravine. On the west is the forest.

'Now then! We start from the front court, a

triangle, with around it the kitchens, stables, and the rooms of the lay brothers and novices. Then we have the temple court, flanked by two squares, which stand for two large, three-storeyed buildings. The west wing has the refectory on the ground floor, the library on the second, and the quarters of the Prior, the almoner and the registrar on the third. The east wing has on the ground floor the large assembly hall where they are now staging the mystery plays, and the offices. The second and third floor are for lodging visitors from outside. You and your family have been accommodated there, I suppose?'

'Yes,' the judge replied, 'we are on the north-east corner of the third floor. Two large, comfortable rooms.'

'Good. We go on. At the back of the temple court is the temple itself – there are some fine antique statues, well worth seeing. Behind the temple is the central court, with a tower on each corner. You are here, in the south-west tower, which was assigned to me. On the left of the court is the Gallery of Horrors – a concession to popular beliefs, Dee! – on the right are the quarters of the ordained monks, and at the back, over the gate, the private residence of the Abbot. Lastly we have a circular section, the Sanctum. To sum up, we have a triangle, two squares, one square, and a circle, in that order. Each of those shapes has a mystical meaning, but we'll skip that. The main thing is that now you know how to orientate yourself. There are, of course, hundreds of passages, corridors and staircases that connect all the buildings, but if you keep this diagram in mind, you can't go far wrong!'

'Thank you, sir!' Judge Dee said gratefully. 'What buildings are there in the sanctum?'

'Only a small pagoda which contains the urn with the ashes of the Founding Saint.'

'Does nobody live in that part of the monastery?'

'Of course not! I visited the place myself, there is only that pagoda and the surrounding wall. But as it is considered the holiest part, I did not draw it in my diagram, so as not to offend our good Abbot. I replaced it by the halved circle you see there on top, the Taoist symbol of the working of the universe. It represents the interaction of the two Primordial Forces, the eternal rhythm of nature which we call Tao. You may call those two forces Light and Dark, Positive and Negative, Man and Woman, Sun and Moon – take your choice! The circle shows how, when Positive reaches its lowest ebb, it merges with Negative, and how when Negative attains its zenith it naturally changes into Positive at its lowest point. The supreme doctrine of Tao, Dee, expressed in one simple symbol!'

'What is the meaning of those two dots inside each half?' Judge Dee asked, interested despite himself.

'It means that Positive harbours the germ of Negative, and vice versa. That applies to all natural phenomena, including man and woman.

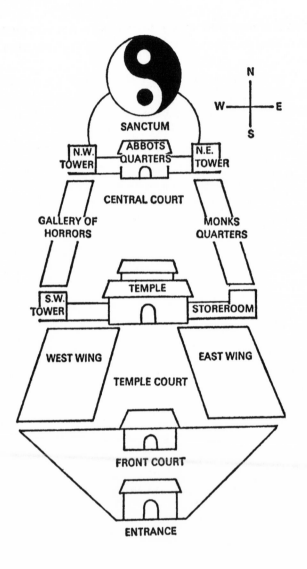

You'll know that every man has in his nature a feminine element, and every woman a masculine strain.'

'That's quite true!' the judge said pensively. Then he added: 'I seem to remember that somewhere I saw that circle also divided horizontally. Does that have a special significance?'

'Not that I know of. The dividing line ought to be vertical, as I drew it here. Well, let's not keep the Abbot waiting. My old friend is rather a stickler for formality!' As they went outside Sun added quickly: 'Mind your step now, the balustrade is broken here. The lay brothers were supposed to repair it, but they maintain that the preparations for the festival kept them too busy. They are a pack of lazybones, anyway! Here, I'll hold your arm, I don't suffer from any fear of heights!'

9

They descended the winding staircase together. It was cold and damp in the stairwell. Judge Dee was glad when they entered the refectory on the ground floor, which was well heated by numerous braziers.

The small Prior came to meet them, nervously blinking his eyes. He fell over his words in a frantic attempt to be exactly as polite to Master Sun as he was to Judge Dee. He conducted them to the main table in the rear of the refectory, where the Abbot was waiting for them. Judge Dee wanted Master Sun to sit on the Abbot's right side, but Sun protested that he was only a retired scholar without official rank, and that the judge, as representative of the Imperial Government, ought to sit in the place of honour. At last the judge had to give in, and the three men seated themselves. The Prior, the almoner and Tsung Lee sat down at a smaller table next to theirs.

The Abbot raised his cup and toasted his two distinguished table companions. This was the sign for the crowd of monks, seated at four long tables in front of them, to take up their chopsticks, which they did with alacrity. Judge Dee noticed that Kuan Lai, his wife and the two actresses were sitting at a separate table near the entrance of the hall, where Tao Gan had joined them. Mo Mo-te was nowhere to be seen.

The judge stared dubiously at the cold, fried fish the Abbot placed on his plate. The bowl of glutinous rice with raisins did not look very attractive either. He had no appetite at all. In order to conceal his lack of enthusiasm he remarked:

'I thought that in Taoist monasteries no meat or fish was served.'

'We do indeed strictly observe the monastic rules,' the Abbot said with a smile. 'We abstain from all intoxicants – my wine-cup is filled with tea. Not yours, though! We make an exception for our honoured guests in this one respect, but we keep strictly to a vegetarian diet. That fish is made of bean curd, and what looks like a roasted chicken over there is moulded from flour and sesame oil.'

Judge Dee was dismayed. He was not a gourmet, but he liked at least to know what he ate. He forced himself to taste a small morsel of the bean-curd fish, and nearly choked. Seeing the Abbot's expectant look, he said quickly:

'This is indeed delicious. You have excellent cooks!'

He quickly emptied his cup, the warm rice wine was not bad. The make-believe fish on his plate stared up at him mournfully with its one shrivelled eye, which was in fact a small dried prune. Somehow or other it made Judge Dee think of the embalmed Abbot. He said:

'After the banquet I would like to see the

temple. And also the crypt under the sanctum, to offer a prayer for the soul of your predecessor.'

The Abbot put his rice bowl down and said slowly:

'This person shall be glad to show Your Honour the temple. But the crypt can unfortunately be opened only on certain days during the dry season. If we open it now, the air down there might get humid, and that would adversely affect the condition of the embalmed body. The intestines have been removed, of course, but some of the organs that remain are still susceptible to decay.'

This technical information robbed the judge of the little appetite he had been able to muster. He quickly drank another cup of wine. The bandage round his head was lessening his throbbing headache, but his body was stiff and painful all over, and he felt slightly sick. He looked with envy at Sun Ming, who was eating with a hearty appetite. When Sun had emptied his bowl, he wiped his mouth with the hot towel a novice handed to him, then said:

'The late Abbot, His Reverence Jade Mirror, was a talented man. He was completely familiar with all the most abstruse texts, wrote a beautiful hand, and was also a good painter of animals and flowers.'

'I would like to see his work,' Judge Dee said politely. 'I suppose the library here has many of his manuscripts and pictures?'

'No,' the Abbot said, 'unfortunately not. It was

his express instruction that all his paintings and writings were to be buried with him in the crypt.'

'Commendable modesty!' Master Sun said with approval. 'But listen, there's that last painting he did of his cat! It is hanging now in the side hall of the temple. I'll take you there after the meal, Dee!'

The judge didn't feel the slightest interest in the late Abbot's cat, and the temple hall would doubtless be stone-cold. But he murmured that he would be delighted.

Sun and the Abbot started with relish on a thick brown broth. Judge Dee poked suspiciously with his chopsticks at the unidentified objects that floated on its surface. He could not muster sufficient courage for tasting the broth. He cudgelled his brain for some more conversation, and at last managed to formulate some intelligent questions about the internal organization of the Taoist church. But the Abbot seemed ill at ease; he disposed of the subject with a few brief explanations.

The judge felt relieved when he saw the Prior, the almoner, and Tsung Lee come to their table to offer a toast. Judge Dee rose and walked back with them to their table to return the courtesy. He sat down opposite the poet, who had apparently partaken liberally of the hot wine. His face was flushed and he seemed in high spirits. The Prior informed the judge that two lay brothers had already replaced the broken axle. The grooms had rubbed down and fed the horses. Thus the distinguished guest would be able to continue his journey the next morning. Unless he decided, of course, to prolong his stay – which would delight the Prior.

Judge Dee thanked him warmly. The Prior muttered some self-deprecatory remarks, then rose and excused himself. He and the almoner had to make preparations for the evening service.

When he was alone with the poet, the judge remarked:

'I don't see Mrs Pao and her daughter here.'

'Daughter?' Tsung Lee asked with a thick tongue. 'Do you seriously sustain the thesis, sir, that such a refined and slender girl can be the daughter of such a vulgar, fat woman?'

'Well,' Judge Dee said non-committally, 'the passing of the years sometimes effects astonishing changes.'

The poet hiccoughed.

'Excuse me!' he said. 'They are trying to poison me with their filthy food. It upsets my stomach. Let me tell you, Magistrate, that Mrs Pao is no lady. The logical conclusion is that White Rose isn't her daughter.' Shaking his forefinger at the judge he asked with a conspiratorial air: 'How do you know that the poor girl isn't being forced to become a nun?'

'I don't,' the judge replied. 'But I can ask her. Where would they be?'

'Probably taking their meal up in their room. Wise precaution too, for a decent girl shouldn't be exposed to the leers of those lewd monks. The fat woman acted wisely, for once!'

'She didn't prevent the girl from being exposed to your gaze, my friend!' Judge Dee remarked.

The poet righted himself, not without difficulty.

'My intentions, sir,' he declared ponderously, 'are strictly honourable!'

'I am glad to hear that!' the judge said dryly. 'By the way, I would have liked to see the crypt you spoke of. But the Abbot informed me just now that it can't be opened at this time of the year.'

Tsung Lee gave the judge a long look from his bleary eyes. Then he said:

'So that's what he told you, eh?'

'Have you been down there yourself?'

The poet looked quickly at the Abbot. Then he said in a low voice:

'Not yet, but I am going to! I think the poor fellow was poisoned! Just as they are trying to poison you and me now! Mark my words!'

'You are drunk!' Judge Dee said contemptuously.

'I don't deny that!' Tsung said placidly. 'It's the only way to stay sane in this mortuary! But let me assure you, sir, that the old Abbot wasn't drunk when he wrote his letter to my father, the last one before he died – I beg your pardon, before he was translated.'

The judge raised his eyebrows.

'Did the old Abbot say in that letter that his life was in danger?' he asked.

Tsung Lee nodded. He drank deeply from his wine-beaker.

'Who did he say was threatening him?' Judge Dee asked again.

The poet set down his beaker hard. He shook his head reprovingly and said:

'You shouldn't try to tempt me to lay myself open to the charge of bringing a false accusation, Magistrate! I know the law!' Leaning over to the judge he whispered portentously: 'Wait till I have collected proof!'

Judge Dee silently caressed his sidewhiskers. The youngster was a disgusting specimen, but his father had been a great man, widely respected in both official and scholarly circles. If the old Abbot had indeed written such a letter to Dr Tsung before he died, the matter deserved further investigation. He asked:

'What is the present Abbot's opinion?'

The poet smiled slyly. Looking at the judge with watery eyes he said:

'You ask him, Magistrate! Perhaps he won't lie to you!'

Judge Dee got up. The youngster was very drunk.

When he had returned to his own table, the Abbot said bitterly:

'I see that Mr Tsung is drunk again. How different he is from his late father!'

'I gather that Dr Tsung was a patron of this monastery,' the judge remarked. He took a sip from the strong tea that indicated the end of the banquet.

'He was indeed,' the Abbot replied. 'A remarkable family, Your Honour! The grandfather was a coolie in a village down south. He used to sit in the street under the window of the village school, and learned to write by tracing in the sand the letters the teacher wrote on the blackboard. After he had passed the village examination, a few shop-keepers collected the money for letting him pursue his studies, and he came out first in the provincial examinations. He was appointed magistrate, married a girl from an impoverished old family, and later died as a Prefect. Dr Tsung was his eldest son, he passed all the examinations with honours, married the daughter of a wealthy tea-merchant, and ended his career as Provincial Governor. He invested his money wisely, and founded the enormous family fortune.'

'It is because every man of talent can rise to the highest functions, regardless of means or social position, that our great Empire will flourish for ever and ever,' Judge Dee said with satisfaction. 'To come back to your predecessor, what disease did he die of?'

The Abbot put down his cup. He replied slowly:

'His Holiness Jade Mirror did not die of a disease. He was translated, that is he chose to leave us because he felt that he had reached the limit set for his stay on earth. He departed for the Isles of the Blest in good health and in full possession of his mental powers. A most remarkable and awe-inspiring miracle that left a lasting impression on all of us who had the privilege of witnessing it.'

'It certainly was a memorable experience, Dee!'

Sun Ming added. 'I was present at it, you know. The Abbot summoned all the elders and, sitting on his high seat, delivered an inspired sermon of nearly two hours. Then he folded his arms, closed his eyes and passed away.'

Judge Dee nodded. The dissolute youngster had evidently been indulging in drunken fantasies. Or perhaps he was repeating false rumours. He said:

'Such a miracle is liable to excite the envy of other sects. One could imagine that the black-robed crowd of the Buddhists would use it for spreading malicious rumours.'

'I certainly wouldn't put it beyond them!' the Abbot said.

'Anyway,' Judge Dee resumed, 'if evil-minded persons ever made slanderous allegations, an autopsy would soon prove them unfounded. Signs of violence can be detected, even on an embalmed body.'

'Let's hope that it'll never come to that!' Sun said cheerfully. 'Well, it's time I returned to my studies.' Getting up he added to the judge: 'I'll first show you that picture of the old Abbot's cat, though! It's a relic of this temple, Dee!'

The judge suppressed a sigh. He thanked the Abbot for the lavish entertainment, then followed Sun to the exit. While passing the actors' table he said quickly to Tao Gan:

'Wait for me in the portal here! I'll be back soon.'

Master Sun walked with the judge through the side corridor, and took him to the west hall of the temple.

Scroll-painting of the Old Abbot's Cat

83

Against the back wall stood a simple altar with four burning candles. Sun lifted one of them and let its light fall on a medium-sized scroll-painting suspended on the wall, mounted with a frame of antique brocade. It was a picture of a long-haired grey cat, lying on the edge of a table of carved ebony. Next to it was a woollen ball, behind it a bronze bowl with a piece of rock of interesting shape, and a few bamboos.

'That was the Abbot's favourite cat, you know!' Sun explained in a low voice. 'The old man painted it countless times. It's rather good, isn't it?'

Judge Dee thought it was very mediocre amateur's work, but he understood that its value lay in its association with the holy man. The side hall was very cold, just as he had feared. 'A remarkable picture!' he said politely.

'It was the last picture he did,' Sun said. 'He painted it up in his room, in the afternoon of the day he died. The cat refused to eat and died a few days later. And to think that people say that cats don't attach themselves to their masters! I advise you now to have a look at the statues of the Taoist Triad in the main hall, they are more than ten foot high – the work of a famous sculptor. I'll be off now, I hope to see you tomorrow morning before you leave.'

Judge Dee respectfully conducted him to the gate of the front hall, then he went back to the refectory. Since the statues had been there for two hundred years, they would be standing there a little longer, he presumed. He could see them when he revisited the temple at some later date.

He found his assistant waiting for him in the portal. He reported in a low voice:

'Mo Mo-te is still missing, sir. Kuan told me that nobody can say when or where he'll turn up, for he likes to go his own way. The director and the others were garrulous enough at table, but they really know very little about what is going on here, and care less. It was a pleasant meal, though. The only discordant note was an altercation at the table of the lay brothers. The brother in charge of the refectory maintained that the others hadn't put enough covers on the table. One monk was complaining that he didn't have a bowl and chop-sticks.'

'You call it a pleasant meal?' Judge Dee asked sourly. 'I only had a few cups of wine and some tea, the rest made my stomach turn!'

'I had a very satisfactory dinner,' Tao Gan said contentedly. 'And all that good food gratis for nothing!'

Judge Dee smiled. He knew that Tao Gan was inclined to be parsimonious. The gaunt man resumed:

'Kuan invited me to come up to his room for a few more drinks, but I think I ought to have a look around for our mysterious actor first.'

'Do that!' the judge said. 'I'll go now and pay a visit to Mrs Pao and her daughter. Their relation to Miss Ou-yang puzzles me. Tsung Lee suggested that White Rose isn't Mrs Pao's daughter, and that she is being forced to become a nun against her will. But the fellow was drunk. He also maintained that the former Abbot had been murdered, but I made inquiries with the Abbot and Master Sun, and that proved to be pure nonsense. Do you know where Mrs Pao's room is?'

'On the second floor, sir, the fifth door in the second corridor, I would say.'

'Good. Let's meet again in Kuan's room. I'll join you there after my talk with Mrs Pao. I don't hear the rain any more, so we can go to the east wing direct by crossing the courtyard.'

But a drenched novice who had just come in informed them that, although the storm had abated somewhat, it was still raining. Thus the judge and Tao Gan made the detour through the front hall of the temple, now crowded with monks. They parted in front of the assembly hall on the ground floor of the east wing.

Judge Dee found the second floor completely deserted. The narrow, cold corridors were scantily lit by an occasional lantern. It was very still; he only heard the rustling of his brocade robe.

He was just about to start counting doors when he thought he heard whispered voices. He stood still and listened. He heard a swishing of silk behind him and at the same time smelled a sweet, cloying perfume. He was about to turn round when suddenly a searing pain shot through his head and everything went black.

10

Judge Dee's first thought was that his cold must have suddenly taken a turn for the worse. His head was aching badly and he had a queer empty feeling in the pit of his stomach. He smelled a faint, feminine perfume. He opened his eyes.

He stared, astonished, at the blue silk curtains above his head. He was lying, fully dressed, in a strange bedstead. He raised his hand to his head and found that his cap and the bandage were gone. There was a large lump on the back of his head. He felt it with his fingertips, and winced.

'Try to take a sip of this!' a soft voice spoke up by his side.

Miss Ting bent over him, a teacup in her hand. She passed her left arm round his shoulders and helped him to sit up. Suddenly he felt very dizzy. She steadied him, and after a few sips of the hot tea he felt somewhat better. Slowly he began to realize what had happened.

'I was knocked down from behind,' he said, looking sourly at her. 'What do you know about that?'

Miss Ting sat down on the edge of the bed. She said placidly:

'I heard a bump against my door. I went to open it and found you lying unconscious on the floor, your head against my door-jamb. Since I thought that signified that you had intended to pay me a visit, I dragged you inside and put you on the bed. Fortunately I am rather strong, for I can assure you that you are by no means a light burden. I wet your temples with cold water till you came to. That's all I know.'

Judge Dee frowned. He asked curtly:

'Who did you see in the corridor?'

'Nobody at all!'

'Did you hear the sound of footsteps?'

'No!'

'Let me see your satchel with perfume!'

Miss Ting obediently loosened the small brocade satchel from her sash and gave it to the judge. He smelled it. It was a sweet perfume, but quite different from the cloying smell he perceived just before he was attacked. He asked again:

'How long have I been unconscious?'

'Quite some time. I would say two hours or so. It's nearly midnight now.' Then she added, pouting: 'Is the verdict guilty or not guilty?'

Judge Dee smiled wanly.

'I am sorry!' he said. 'I was a bit confused. You were very kind, Miss Ting. If it hadn't been for you, the rascal who knocked me down would doubtless have finished me off then and there.'

'It was the bandage under your cap that saved your life,' Miss Ting remarked. 'They must have hit you a vicious blow with something sharp, and if you hadn't been wearing that thick bandage filled with orange peel round your head, the blow would have cracked your skull.'

'I ought to go up and thank my wives!' Judge Dee muttered. 'It was they who insisted on my wearing the bandage. But I must first look into this treacherous attack!' He wanted to climb down from the bed, but a sudden attack of dizziness forced him to lie down again.

'Not so quick, Magistrate!' Miss Ting said. 'It was a nasty blow. I'll help you to get down and over to that armchair there.'

When the judge was sitting at the rickety table, she dipped the bandage in the brass water-basin on the dressing-table. 'I'll put this round your head again,' she remarked, 'it'll help to make the lump go down.'

Sipping his tea, Judge Dee looked thoughtfully at her pleasant, frank face. She was not particularly handsome, but decidedly attractive. He put her age at about twenty-five. The straight robe of black silk with the broad red sash set off her narrow waist and small, firm breasts. She had the lithe, supple body of the trained acrobat. After she had wound the bandage round his head and replaced his cap, the judge said:

'Sit down and let's talk a little, while I am getting ready to go. Tell me, why did you, a nice-looking and capable young girl, choose this particular profession? I don't consider it dishonourable, mind you, but I'd have thought that a girl like you could easily have found a better way of life.'

She shrugged her shoulders. Pouring out another cup of tea for the judge, she answered:

'Oh, I fear that I am a rather wayward and self-willed person. My father has a small pharmacy in the capital, and also five daughters, worse luck! I am the eldest, and father wanted to sell me as a concubine to the retail drug-dealer, to whom he owed money. I thought the dealer was a nasty old man, but the alternative was a brothel and I didn't fancy that either. I had always been rather strong and fond of sports, so, with my father's permission, I joined Kuan's troupe. Kuan advanced the money my father needed. I soon learned to act, and also to do acrobatic dances and juggling. After one year Kuan had the loan back, plus the interest. Kuan is a decent fellow, he never made passes at me or forced me to grant my favours to patrons of our show. So I stayed on.' She wrinkled her nose as she went on: 'I know that people say all actors are crooks and all actresses whores, but I can assure you that Kuan is scrupulously honest. And as regards myself, though I don't claim to lead a saintly life, I never sold my body and I never will.'

Judge Dee nodded. He resumed:

'You say that Kuan never bothered you, but what about Mo Mo-te?'

'Well, he did make a few passes at me in the beginning, but rather because he felt it was his duty as a man than because he really wanted me; I could feel that immediately. Yet he took my refusal badly, it hurt his stupid pride. He has been unpleasant to me ever since, which I regret, for he is a superb swordsman and I would have liked to do an act with him.'

'I didn't like the way he threatened Miss Ou-yang on the stage,' the judge remarked. 'Do you think Mo is the type of man who takes delight in inflicting pain on a woman?'

'Oh no! He has a violent temper, but he is not mean or nasty. You can take that from me, and I know a thing or two about men!'

'Did Miss Ou-yang jilt him too?'

Miss Ting hesitated. She replied slowly:

'Miss Ou-yang has joined our troupe only recently, you see, and . . .'

Her voice trailed off. She quickly emptied her teacup. Then she took a chopstick from the table, threw the saucer up in the air and caught it on its tip, where she made the saucer whirl round expertly.

'Put that down!' the judge said, annoyed. 'It makes me dizzy all over again!' And when she had skilfully caught the saucer and put it back on the table he added: 'Answer my question! Did Ou-yang jilt Mo Mo-te?'

'You needn't shout at me!' Miss Ting said stiffly. 'I was just coming to that. Miss Ou-yang is a bit too fond of me, you know. I don't go for that sort of thing, so I keep her at a distance. But Mo is convinced that we are having an affair, that's why he is jealous and hates her.'

'I see. How long has Mo been with the show?'

'About one year. I don't think he is really an

actor, but a vagabond who roams all over the Empire, making his living in various ways. At any rate I don't think Mo is his real name. I once saw a jacket of his marked with the name Liu, but he maintained he had bought it in a pawnshop. And another thing, he must have visited this monastery before.'

'How do you know that?' the judge asked eagerly.

'On our first day here he already knew his way about quite well. We all think this a creepy place and keep to our own rooms as much as possible, but Mo wanders about all by himself most of the time and isn't at all afraid of getting lost in this rabbit-warren.'

'You'd better be careful with him,' Judge Dee said gravely. 'He may be a criminal, for all we know. I am also worrying about Miss Ou-yang.'

'You don't think she might be a criminal too, do you?' Miss Ting asked quickly.

'No, but I feel I ought to know a little more about her.'

He looked expectantly at the girl. She hesitated a few moments then said:

'I promised Kuan I wouldn't tell anybody, but after all you are the magistrate here, and that makes it different. Besides, I wouldn't like you to suspect Miss Ou-yang of some evil designs. She is not really an actress, and Ou-yang isn't her real name. I don't know who she is. I only know that she is from the capital, and a wealthy woman. She paid Kuan a large sum for offering his services to this monastery for the commemoration festival, and for letting her join his troupe during their stay here. She assured Kuan that her only purpose was to warn someone here, and that therefore she wanted to perform an act on the stage with her bear, and that she would choose her own make-up. Kuan didn't see any objection to that, and, since it would mean a double profit for us, he agreed. After our arrival here she didn't take part in our sessions with the monks, she left it to Kuan, his wife and me to teach those blockheads how to move about on the stage. Mo wasn't a great help either, for that matter.'

'Do you think Mo knew Miss Ou-yang before?' the judge asked quickly.

'That I don't know. When they are together they are mostly quarrelling with each other. Well, tonight we saw that she had made herself up so as to resemble Miss Pao, and later Kuan asked her about it but she said only that she knew what she was doing. When you came unexpectedly to see Kuan he got very frightened, because he thought that Miss Ou-yang had been up to something illegal, and that you had come to investigate. That's all, but please don't let Kuan or the others know that I told you.'

Judge Dee nodded. He thought ruefully that this strange tale complicated matters still further. He got up from his chair but suddenly felt very ill. He motioned to Miss Ting that he wished to be left alone and stumbled to the night-commode in the corner. He vomited violently.

After he had washed his face in the basin on the dressing-table and combed his beard, he felt much better. He drank a cup of tea, then went to the door and called Miss Ting in. He found that he could walk steadily now, and his headache was gone. He said with a smile:

'I'll be on my way now. Thanks again for your timely assistance. If ever I can do anything to help you, let me know. I am bad at forgetting!'

Miss Ting nodded. She lowered her eyes and played for a while with the ends of her red sash. Suddenly she looked up and said:

'I'd like to ask your advice about ... about a rather personal matter. It's a bit awkward, but as a judge you must hear many things people are not supposed to talk about. Anyway, to put it plainly, I didn't enjoy the few love-affairs I had as much as a girl is supposed to do. But I must confess I do feel very much attracted to Miss Ou-yang, more than to any man I ever met. I keep telling myself that it's all nonsense and that it will pass. I purposely keep out of her way. But at the same time I am worrying whether perhaps I am by nature unfit for marriage. I would hate to make a man who married me unhappy, you know. What do you think I should do?'

Judge Dee began to scratch his head, but a sharp pain made him desist hurriedly. He slowly tugged at his moustache instead. Then he said:

'I would do nothing, for the time being. Maybe you didn't really like the men you associated with before, or maybe they didn't really like you. At any rate those temporary liaisons can never be compared with married life. Continued intimacy fosters mutual understanding, and that is the basis of a happy love-life. Moreover, Miss Ou-yang is a bit mysterious, and that, together with the flattering attention she pays to you, may also account for the attraction you feel. So go on keeping her at a distance, till you know more about your own feelings, and about her intentions. Don't rush into an adventure that may lessen your self-respect and warp your emotions, unless you are completely sure of yourself and of the other party. Speaking now as your magistrate, I can add only that, since both of you are grown-up and free women, your love-life is no concern of mine; the law intervenes only when minors or dependants are involved. To let everybody arrange his private life as he likes, provided he doesn't injure others or prejudice legally defined relationships – that is the spirit of our society and the laws that govern it.'

'That man Tsung Lee always makes unpleasant references to Miss Ou-yang and me!' Miss Ting said unhappily.

'Don't mind him, he is an irresponsible youngster. By the way, he has a theory that Miss Pao is being forced to become a nun.'

'Nonsense!' Miss Ting exclaimed. 'I had some talks with her alone, her room is on this same floor. She is very keen on entering a nunnery. She gave me to understand that she had an unhappy love-affair and that she therefore wished to retire from worldly life.'

'I was on my way to Mrs Pao when I was attacked,' the judge said. 'Now it is too late. I'll visit them tomorrow morning. Is Mo's room also on this floor?'

'Yes, it is.' She counted on her fingers, then continued: 'Mo's room is the fourth on your right, after you have turned the corner.'

'Again many thanks!' Judge Dee said as he turned to the door. 'And don't worry about yourself!'

She gave him a grateful smile, and he went outside.

11

He quickly looked up and down the corridor. It seemed unlikely that his attacker would dare to lie in wait for a second attempt, but one never knew. However, all was silent as the grave. He walked down the corridor, deep in thought.

That rascal Mo Mo-te was tall and strong enough to have dealt him the blow. And as to motive, if Mo was a maniac who chose women as his victims, and if he had been the actor who had come barging into the reception room during his conversation with the Abbot, Mo might well have feared that he, the judge, was about to investigate irregularities with girls in the monastery, and thus trace Mo's doings with that one-armed woman – if the scene he had witnessed hadn't been a hallucination! At any rate he ought to ask the Abbot which actor had intruded on them during their talk in the reception room.

What Miss Ting had told him about Miss Ou-yang worried him also. The girl had evidently made herself up to resemble Miss Pao in order to warn her or her mother. But against what or whom? Probably Miss Ou-yang had lied to Kuan; it was a preposterous idea that a wealthy girl from the capital would keep an enormous bear as a pet. It was far more likely that Miss Ou-yang was a member of some travelling show, who had joined Kuan's troupe on the orders of a third person, as yet unknown. It was all very confusing.

Shaking his head disconsolately Judge Dee rounded the corner. He halted in front of the fourth door on the left. He knocked, but, as he had expected, there was no answer. He pushed against the door and found that it was not locked. This was the opportunity to search Mo Mo-te's personal effects.

When he had opened the door he vaguely saw a table with a candle, in front of a large cupboard, the door of which was open. He stepped inside and closed the door behind him, then walked over to the table, feeling in his sleeve for his tinder-box. Suddenly he heard a deep growl behind him.

He swung round. By the door, close to the floor, a pair of green eyes were staring fixedly at him. They slowly rose, then the judge felt the floor-boards tremble under a heavy tread.

His way to the door was cut off. He quickly felt his way round the table and frantically groped in the dark for the door of the cupboard he had seen. He found it and stepped inside, pulling the door shut behind him. He heard the growling very near, on the other side. There was the sound of scratching nails. Then the growling grew louder.

Judge Dee cursed his absent-mindedness. He now remembered too late, that Miss Ting had spoken about the fourth door on the *right*. He had entered by mistake the room opposite, evidently that of Miss Ou-yang. She was out, but that awful brute was there.

The scratching stopped. The planks under Judge Dee's feet shook as the bear lay down in front of the cupboard.

This was a most unpleasant situation. Presumably Miss Ou-yang would arrive before long, and he could shout at her through the door. But in the meantime he was at the mercy of that fearsome creature. He hadn't the slightest idea of the behaviour of bears. Would the animal presently try to smash the door? It seemed solid enough, but if the bear threw his enormous weight against it, he could doubtless easily smash the entire cupboard to pieces.

The cupboard was empty, but there wasn't much space. He had to stand half-bent, the ceiling-boards pressed down painfully on the lump on the back of his head. And the air was getting very close. Soon it would become suffocating. He carefully opened the door a narrow crack.

A waft of fresh air came inside, but at the same moment there was a commotion outside that made the cupboard shake. The bear growled ominously, and began again to scratch at the door. The judge closed it quickly and kept both hands on the handle.

A cold fear gripped his heart. This was a situation he was utterly unable to cope with. Soon the stale air was hurting his lungs, sweat broke out all over his body. If he put the door ajar again, would the bear push his paw inside and force it open?

Just when he had decided that he would have to risk it again, he heard someone enter the room. A voice said gruffly:

'Are you after the mice again? Back to your corner, quick!'

The floor shook again under the bear's heavy tread. The judge opened the door very slightly and filled his lungs with fresh air. He saw Miss Ou-yang lighting the candle. Then she went up to the dressing-table, took a handful of sugared fruit from a drawer and threw it to the bear.

'Well caught!' she said. The bear growled.

Judge Dee heaved a deep sigh of relief. He didn't relish the task ahead of announcing his presence from his undignified hide-out, but anything was better than being mauled by that fearful brute! He opened his mouth to speak, then saw to his embarrassment that Miss Ou-yang had untied her sash and was now impatiently tugging at her robe. He would have to wait until she had changed into her night-dress. He was about to pull the door shut again when he suddenly halted. He looked wide-eyed at the girl's bare arms. They were thin, but there was a rippling movement of well-developed muscles, and the upper arms were covered with black hair. There was a long red scar on the left arm. The robe fell down and revealed the bare torso of a young man.

The judge opened the door wider. He cleared his throat and said:

100

'I am the magistrate, I entered here by mistake.'
As the bear lumbered forward with an angry
growl he quickly added: 'Keep that beast away
from me!'

The young man at the dressing-table looked,
dumbfounded, at the figure in the cupboard. Then
he barked an order at the bear. It went back to its
corner by the window, still growling. Its neck hairs
stood on end.

'You can come out!' the youngster said curtly.
'He won't touch you.'

Judge Dee stepped into the room and went to
the chair by the table, eyeing the bear suspiciously.

'Sit down!' the other exclaimed impatiently. 'I
tell you it's safe!'

'Even so, I want you to put him on the chain!'
the judge said curtly.

The youngster took off his wig, then went up
to the bear and attached a heavy chain to its iron
collar. The other end was fastened to a hook in
the window-sill. Judge Dee thought that the snap
of the lock was one of the nicest sounds he had
ever heard. He sat down on the bamboo chair.

The young man put on a loose jacket. He sat
down too and said in a surly voice:

'Well, now you have found me out, what are
you going to do about it?'

'You are Miss Pao's brother, aren't you?' the
judge asked.

'I am. But fortunately that woman Pao isn't my
mother! How did you know?'

'When watching your act,' Judge Dee replied,

'it struck me that White Rose was very frightened when Mo Mo-te threatened you with his sword, while your scene with the bear left her completely unperturbed. That indicated that she knew everything about you and your bear. And when just now I saw your face I noticed that there's a basic resemblance.'

The young man nodded.

'Anyway,' he said, 'I have committed only the minor offence of posing as a member of the other sex. And in a good cause.'

'You'd better tell me all about it. Who are you?'

'I am Kang I-te, eldest son of Kang Woo, the well-known rice merchant in the capital. White Rose is my only sister. Half a year ago she fell in love with a young student, but my father disapproved of the match and refused to give his consent to the marriage. Soon after that the young fellow fell off his horse when returning drunk from a party. He broke his back and died on the spot. My sister was brokenhearted. She maintained that her sweetheart had become despondent because of my father's refusal, and that my parents were responsible for his taking to drink, and thus for his death. That was nonsense, because the fellow was a drunkard to begin with. But you try to reason with a girl in love! White Rose announced that she would enter religion. Father and Mother did what they could to persuade her to give up that plan, but that only made her all the more stubborn. She threatened to kill herself if they didn't let her go. She entered the White Crane Nunnery in the capital as a novice.'

Kang rubbed his upper lip, where he had evidently worn a moustache, and continued unhappily:

'I went there several times and tried to reason with her. I explained to her that the young man had been notorious for his dissolute life, and that Father had been quite right in opposing the marriage. The only result was that she grew furious with me and refused to see me again. Last time I went there the Abbess told me that White Rose had left, and that she didn't know where she had gone. I bribed the gate-keeper, and he told me that a certain Mrs Pao, a pious widow, had struck up a friendship with her and taken her away. My parents were worried, and my father ordered me to make further inquiries. By dint of much effort I at last discovered that Mrs Pao had taken my sister to this monastery, to be initiated as a nun. I decided to follow her in order to try again to persuade my sister to return home. Since I knew she would refuse to see me if I went as I was, I disguised myself as an actress. I am of rather slight build, and I have taken part in some amateur theatricals. As Miss Ou-yang I approached Kuan, and bribed him to offer his services to this monastery for the commemoration festival and to let me join his troupe. The fellow acted in good faith, you shouldn't blame him, sir.

'The stratagem worked. Mo Mo-te unwittingly did me a service when he teased me during his sword-dance. It frightened my sister and made her forget her resentment against me. After the show she slipped away from Mrs Pao and hurriedly told me behind the stage that she was in an awful quandary. Mrs Pao had been very kind to her, she had more or less adopted her as her daughter. Her one great aim in life was to see my sister properly ordained as a nun, for she was a very pious woman. However, in this monastery White Rose had met a young fellow, a certain Mr Tsung. Though she didn't know him yet very well, her meeting him had made her doubt whether after all she had taken the right decision. But on the other hand she could never disappoint Mrs Pao, who had gone to so much trouble for her, and who had consoled her when her own family had turned against her. Those were the words she used, "turned against her". I ask you, sir! Well, I said she had better come up to my room for a quiet talk about what she should do. I told her to take off her black dress; in her white undergarment people would take her for me. She did so and then went away, stuffing her folded black robe in her sleeve.'

He scratched his head and resumed ruefully:

'I was going to follow her upstairs, but in the hall I ran into that fool Tsung. When I had got rid of him and gone up to my room, my sister wasn't there. I went to Mrs Pao's room, but found nobody there. Then I had a few drinks with Kuan Lai. Just now I went to Mrs Pao's room again, on the off-chance that one of them would still be up. But the lights were out and the door locked. Tomorrow I'll try again. That's all, sir.'

Judge Dee slowly caressed his sidewhiskers. He had heard about Kang Woo, he was indeed a well-known merchant in the capital. He said:

'You would have done better if you had placed this matter in the hands of the proper authorities, Kang.'

'I beg to differ, sir. White Rose is entering religion with my parents' consent, and Mrs Pao is highly thought of in Taoist circles in the capital. And you know, sir, that the Taoists have much influence in government circles nowadays. My father is a Confucianist, but as a merchant he could not afford to become known as an anti-Taoist; it would be bad for his business.'

'Anyway,' Judge Dee said, 'from now on you'll leave this matter to me. Tomorrow morning I'll speak personally with Mrs Pao and your sister. I shall be glad to try to make her come back on her decision, and her interest in Mr Tsung will probably help. I wouldn't choose him for my own son-in-law, but he has a good background and he may improve with the years. Anyway, I hold that Heaven has assigned to woman the duty of marrying and bearing children, I don't hold with nuns, whether Taoist or Buddhist. Now tell me, how did you get this awful animal, and why did you bring him along here?'

'I am fond of hunting, sir. I caught him seven years ago up north, when he was still a small cub. He has been with me ever since; it has been very interesting to teach him dancing and other tricks. He is very fond of me, considers me almost as the father-bear! Only once he lacerated my left arm with his paw, but that was by mistake. It was meant as a caress! It healed well, it only gives me trouble in humid weather like we are having today, then the arm is a bit stiff. When I joined Kuan's troupe I took the bear along, in the first place because he only obeys me and at home no one else can look after him, and secondly because it gave me a good act in Kuan's show.'

The judge nodded. All the pieces were falling into place now. On the stage Kang had made little use of his left arm because the scar was bothering him, and when he and Tao Gan had met White Rose in the corridor, she had kept her left arm close to her body because of the black dress tucked away in her sleeve. And she had been in a great hurry because she didn't want to meet Mrs Pao. She must have met her round the corner, and decided to defer the talk with her brother till next day. He resumed:

'I know next to nothing about bears. What would he have done if you hadn't come? Do you think he would have smashed the cupboard to get at me?'

'Oh no! They are cunning enough, but not very enterprising. They don't do things they have never attempted before, unless they are taught to do them. That's why I can leave him here in this room off the chain, he'll never try to get the door open. He would have sniffed and scratched at that cup-

106

board from time to time to make sure that you were still there, then he would have curled up in front and waited till you came out. They have an infinite patience.'

Judge Dee shivered involuntarily.

'They don't devour people, do they?' he asked.

'Worse than that!' Kang said with a wry smile. 'They'll knock a man down and maul him, then play with him as a cat plays with a mouse till he is dead. I once saw the remains of a hunter who had been torn to pieces by a bear. It wasn't a pretty sight!'

'Good Heavens!' Judge Dee exclaimed. 'What a nice play-mate!'

Kang shrugged his shoulders.

'I never had any trouble with him,' he said. 'He also likes my sister, though he doesn't obey her as he does me. But he hates strangers, they make him nervous. He is quite funny that way, though. Some strangers he doesn't mind, he just gives them one look, then curls up in a corner and ignores them. Evidently you don't come into that category, sir! But I must say that he is in a bad temper now because he doesn't get enough exercise. Later, a couple of hours before dawn, the only time that this bee-hive is quiet, I shall take him to the well between this building and the next. There are no doors or windows on the ground floor there, and the alley is closed by a solid gate; it was used formerly as a kind of prison for offending monks, I heard. There he can exercise a bit without danger to anybody.'

Judge Dee nodded. Then he resumed:

'By the way, have you perhaps seen Mo Mo-te while looking for Mrs Pao and your sister?'

'I did not!' Kang said angrily. 'That rascal is always bothering Miss Ting. I had to keep to my disguise, else I would have given him a thrashing he would remember! He may be taller and heavier than I, but I am a trained boxer and I'll lick him! Now I'll see to it that he keeps away from Miss Ting. That's a fine girl, sir, and good at sports too. She can ride a horse, better indeed than many a man! If she married me I could take her with me on my hunting trips! I have no use for those delicate, pampered damsels my parents are always urging me to marry. But she is very independent, I doubt whether she would have me!'

Judge Dee rose.

'Ask her!' he said. 'You'll find her a very outspoken girl. I must be going now, my assistant will be looking for me.'

He tried a friendly nod at the bear, but the animal only glared at him with its mean small eyes.

12

As soon as Mr Kang had closed the door, Judge Dee stepped up to the one opposite. It was not locked. But when he had pushed it open he saw that nobody was there. A spluttering candle stood on the bamboo table; it had nearly burned out. Except for a made-up bed and two chairs there was no other furniture. There were no boxes or bundles, and not a single garment hung on the wooden clothes rack. If it had not been for the burning candle one would not have thought that anyone was staying there.

The judge pulled the drawer out, but it contained nothing but dust. He went down on his knees and looked under the bed. There was nothing but a small mouse that scurried away.

He got up, dusted his knees and went out, making for Tao Gan's room. It was well past midnight. He supposed that his gaunt assistant would have grown tired of keeping the actors company.

He found Tao Gan sitting alone in his chilly, bare room, hunched over a brazier that contained only two or three glowing coals. Tao Gan hated spending more than absolutely necessary. His long, gloomy face lit up when he saw the judge enter. Rising he asked quickly:

'What happened, Your Honour? I looked every-where but – '

'Give me a cup of hot tea!' Judge Dee said curtly. 'Do you happen to have anything to eat here?'

While Judge Dee sat down heavily at the small table, Tao Gan quickly rummaged through his travelling-box and found two dried oil-cakes. He handed them to the judge, saying dubiously:

'I am sorry I have nothing else to . . .'

The judge took a quick bite.

'They are excellent!' he said contentedly. 'No vegetarian nonsense about these, they have the nice flavour of pork fat!'

After he had munched the cakes and drunk three cups of tea, he yawned and remarked:

'The only thing I want now is a good long sleep! But, although some of our problems are solved, there are still a few things that need our urgent attention. Including an attempted murder!' He told Tao Gan what had happened, and gave him an outline of his talks with Miss Ting and with the pseudo Miss Ou-yang. 'So you see,' he concluded, 'that the case of the pious maid, White Rose, is practically finished. Tomorrow morning, before we leave here, I shall have a talk with her and Mrs Pao. There remains the problem of who hit me on the head and why!'

Tao Gan sat deep in thought, winding and unwinding on his forefinger the three long hairs that sprouted from his left cheek. At last he said:

'Miss Ting told you that Mo Mo-te is familiar with the monastery. Could he perhaps be really a vagrant Taoist monk? Those fellows roam all over the Empire, visiting famous Taoist sites and engaging in all kinds of mischief on the side. Since they don't shave their heads like the Buddhists, they can easily act the part of laymen. Mo Mo-te may have visited this monastery before, probably he became involved in the deaths of one or more of the three girls. The one-armed woman you saw may be another of his victims. Suppose he now came back disguised as an actor, either to silence the one-armed girl, or to blackmail accomplices here?'

'There's much in what you say, Tao Gan,' Judge Dee said pensively. 'It agrees with a vague theory I had been trying to formulate myself. It reminds me of your remark about one cover being missing at the banquet. That might mean that Mo has resumed his Taoist garb and mixed with the monks. If he had an accomplice here, he could easily manage that. The inhabitants of the monastery saw him wearing a mask most of the time, or with his face painted. That would explain also why we can't find him, and why his room is completely empty, as I saw just now. And if it was he who overhead my talk with the Abbot, he might well want me out of the way.'

'But murdering a magistrate is no small undertaking!' Tao Gan remarked.

'That's exactly why Mo is our most likely suspect. I don't think that anyone living in this monastery would dare to do that. Everybody knows that the murder of an Imperial official sets our whole administrative machine into motion, and this monastery would in no time be swarming with investigators, police-officers and special agents who would literally leave no brick unturned to find the criminal. But Mo is an outsider, he'll disappear as soon as he has done whatever he came to do, and little does he care what happens afterwards to the monastery and its inmates!'

Tao Gan nodded his agreement. After a while he spoke:

'We must also keep in mind another possibility, sir. You told me that at the banquet you made inquiries regarding the death of the former Abbot. Now, suppose there had indeed been something wrong about the old fellow's demise, and that someone who had been concerned in that crime overheard your questions. Isn't it then to be expected that he wanted to prevent you at all cost from initiating an investigation?'

'Impossible! I tell you that more than a dozen people were present when the old Abbot died. I said clearly to the Abbot that I didn't believe that . . .' He suddenly broke off. Then he went on slowly: 'Yes, you are perfectly right! I also said that signs of violence can often be detected even on an embalmed corpse. Someone may have heard that, and wrongly concluded that I was thinking of having an autopsy conducted.' He paused. Then he hit his fist on the table and muttered: 'Tsung must tell me all the details about the old Abbot's death! Where can we find that confounded poet?'

'When I left Kuan Lai they were still drinking happily. Probably Tsung Lee is still there. The office paid the actors their fee tonight, and these people like to keep late hours!'

'Good, let's go there.' Getting up the judge added: 'Either that blow on my head, or the couple of hours of enforced rest after it, must have cured my cold! My head is clear now and I have got rid of that feverish feeling. What about you, though?'

'Oh,' Tao Gan said with his thin smile, 'I am all right! I never sleep much, I usually pass the night dozing a bit and thinking about this and that.'

Judge Dee gave his assistant a curious look as the elderly man carefully doused the candle with his nimble fingers. During the years this strange, sad man had been working for him as one of his assistants he had grown rather fond of him. He wondered what he could be thinking of at night. He opened the door.

That same moment he heard the rustling of silk. A dark shape hurried away through the corridor.

'You guard the stairs!' he barked at Tao Gan. He rushed towards the corner round which the unknown listener had disappeared.

Tao Gan ran quickly to the staircase, taking a roll of black waxed thread from his sleeve. As he was stringing it across the stairs, a foot above the first step, he muttered with a sly smile: 'Oh dear, oh dear! If our visitor comes rushing along here I am afraid he'll have a very bad fall!'

Just when he had fastened both ends to the banister, the judge came back.

'No use!' he said bitterly. 'There's a narrow staircase on the other side of the building!'

'What did he look like, sir?'

'I only caught a glimpse of him when I stepped outside. He was round the corner like a flash, and when I got there he was nowhere to be seen. But it was the same villain who attacked me!'

'How does Your Honour know that?' Tao Gan asked eagerly.

'He left behind a whiff of that same sweet perfume I noticed just before I was knocked down,' the judge replied. He tugged at his beard, then said angrily: 'Look here, I am sick and tired of this game of hide and seek! We must do something quickly, because that rascal may have overheard everything we said just now. We'll first go to Kuan's room. If Tsung isn't there, I'll go straight to Master Sun and rouse him. We'll organize a posse to search every nook and cranny of this place, forbidden to visitors or not! Come along!'

Upon entering the actors' dressing-room they found only the director and Tsung Lee. The table bore an impressive array of empty wine-jars. Kuan had passed out, he was lying back in his armchair snoring loudly. Tsung Lee sat hunched over the table, aimlessly drawing figures with his forefinger in the spilt wine. He would have got up when he saw the judge enter, but the latter said curtly:

'Remain seated!'

Taking the chair next to the young man, he went on harshly:

'Listen, you! An attempt on my life was made, it may be connected with your talking about the former Abbot's death. I refuse to be made to run around in circles any longer, I want to hear, here and now, everything you know about that affair. Speak up!'

Tsung Lee passed his hand over his face. The unexpected arrival of the judge and his man, and the harsh address, seemed to have sobered him somewhat. He looked unhappily at the judge, cleared his throat and said hesitantly:

'It's an odd story, sir, I really don't know . . .'

'Stop beating about the bush!' Judge Dee barked. And, to Tao Gan: 'See whether these two tipplers have left anything in those jars and pour me a cup. It'll help me to stay awake!'

The poet looked wistfully at the cup Tao Gan was filling, but the thin man made no move to include him. He sighed and began:

'You must know that my father was a close friend of Jade Mirror, the former Abbot. He often visited this monastery, and they corresponded regularly with each other. In his last letter the Abbot wrote that he didn't trust True Wisdom, the present Abbot, who was then Prior here. Jade Mirror hinted vaguely at irregularities with girls who had come to stay here to be initiated, and – '

'What kind of irregularities?' the judge interrupted sharply.

'He didn't express himself clearly, sir. It seems he suspected that monks tempted those girls to take part in some sort of secret rites, a kind of religious orgy, you know. And he thought, apparently, that the Prior connived at those goings on. He also wrote that he had discovered that the Prior secretly planted nightshades in a hidden corner of the garden. That made Jade Mirror suspect that he was planning to poison somebody.'

Judge Dee set down his wine-beaker hard on the table. He asked angrily:

'Why in Heaven's name weren't those things reported to the magistrate? How can we acquit ourselves of our duties when people keep things hidden from us or tell only half-truths?'

'My father was a very conscientious man, Your Honour,' the poet said apologetically. 'He wouldn't dream of taking any official steps before he had ascertained all the facts. Since during his visits to the monastery Jade Mirror had never referred to those matters, and since the Abbot was over seventy, he reckoned with the possibility that the old man was perhaps seeing things that weren't there; his mind was none too clear, sometimes. My father thought nothing ought to be done before Jade Mirror's vague allegations had been verified. He didn't even want to consult Master Sun without tangible proof. Unfortunately my father fell ill just at that time, and he died before he could do anything about it. But on his deathbed he enjoined me to go and make discreet inquiries here.'

Tsung Lee heaved a sigh, then went on:

'After my father's demise I was fully occupied for several months with putting the family affairs in order. I am the eldest son, you know. Then there arose a complicated dispute about some land we own, and the law-suit dragged on for months. Thus one year passed by before I could come here and start my investigation. I have been at it now for two weeks, but I can't say I have made any progress. Three girls died here, but, as you doubtless know, these deaths had natural explanations. There's not the slightest indication that these young women were used for some unholy experiments. As regards the death of Jade Mirror, I was hampered in my work by the fact that the area north of the temple is closed to visitors. And I wanted especially to visit the crypt to have a look at the papers the dead Abbot left. At last I decided I would try to frighten the Abbot, in the forlorn hope that, if he was guilty, he would give himself away, or take some imprudent steps against me. Hence my poem about the 'deadly shades of night', and about the two abbots. You'll have noticed, sir, that the Abbot was very annoyed.'

'So was I,' Judge Dee remarked dryly, 'and I haven't the murder of an abbot on my conscience. That doesn't mean anything.' He thought for a moment, then resumed: 'During the banquet True Wisdom gave me a brief account of the manner in which the old Abbot died. Tell me all you know about that!'

Tsung Lee cast a longing look at the wine-cup in Judge Dee's hand.

'Give him a cup!' the judge said sourly to Tao

Gan. 'The wick is dry, so the lamp needs oil, it seems.'

The poet gratefully took a long draught, then continued:

'Since Jade Mirror's death was considered a miraculous event all details have been placed on record, to be incorporated in the history of this monastery. About one year ago, on the sixteenth day of the eighth moon, Jade Mirror stayed in his own room all morning. He was alone, and presumably he had been reading the scriptures, as he often did in the morning. He took his noon meal in the refectory, together with True Wisdom, Sun Ming, and the other monks. Thereafter he returned to his own room, together with True Wisdom, for a cup of tea. Soon after that, True Wisdom came out and told the two monks who were standing in the corridor outside that the Abbot wanted to devote the afternoon to painting a picture of his cat.'

'Master Sun showed me that picture,' Judge Dee said. 'It is hanging now in the side hall of the temple.'

'Yes, sir. The old Abbot was very fond of cats, and he liked painting them. True Wisdom returned to the temple. The two monks knew that the old Abbot didn't like to be disturbed when he was painting. Since they were on duty that day in the Abbot's quarters, they remained waiting outside his door to be on hand if he should call them. For an hour or so they heard the Abbot hum some of his favourite religious chants, as was his wont when he was painting and the work got on well. Then he began to speak loudly, as if he was engaged in a dispute with someone. As his voice grew louder and louder, the monks became worried and went inside. They found the Abbot sitting in his armchair, an exalted look on his face. He had left the picture lying on his desk, nearly finished. He ordered the monks to summon Master Sun, the Prior, the almoner and the twelve eldest monks. He said he had an important message for them.

'When all had assembled before the Abbot he smiled happily and announced that Heaven had revealed to him a new formulation of the Truth of Tao, and that he wanted to impart that to them. Sitting upright in his chair with his cat on his lap, he then delivered with flashing eyes a very mystic sermon, couched in strange, obscure language. One of the monks noted it down while he was speaking. Later the text was published, together with an extensive commentary by the Chief Abbot from the capital, who elucidated all the obscure expressions and proved that this was indeed a masterly summing up of the deepest mysteries. Sermon and commentary are now used as basic text in all the monasteries of this province.

'The Abbot spoke for more than two hours. Then suddenly he closed his eyes and leaned back in his chair. His breathing became irregular, then ceased altogether. He was dead.

'All present were deeply moved. Seldom had there been so perfect an example of a Taoist adept of his own will peacefully translating himself from this world to the next. The Chief Abbot in the capital declared Jade Mirror a holy man. His body was embalmed and enshrined in the crypt with magnificent ceremonies that lasted three days and were attended by thousands of people.

'So you see, sir,' Tsung Lee concluded dejectedly, 'that there were more than a dozen witnesses who can attest that the old Abbot died a natural death, and that he did not once refer to his life having been threatened, by True Wisdom or anybody else. I am more and more inclined to think that, when the old man wrote his last letter, his mind was wandering. I told you that he was more than seventy years old, and it was known that he behaved a bit strangely, at times.'

Judge Dee made no comment. He remained silent for a long while, playing with his sidewhiskers. It was very quiet in the room; the only sound heard was the soft snoring of the director. At last the judge spoke:

'We must remember that the old Abbot suggested in his letter that True Wisdom was planning to poison someone with the seeds of the nightshade. Now our medical books state that this poison will bring the victim into a state of extreme exaltation before the coma sets in and he dies. The behaviour of the Abbot during his last hours could conceivably be interpreted from this angle. The old Abbot might well have ascribed his exaltation to the inspiration of Heaven, and forgotten all about his suspicions of True Wisdom. The only objection to this theory is that the Abbot, before summoning the others to hear his last sermon, had been quietly working an hour or so on that picture of his cat. We shall investigate this immediately. Do you know how to get to the crypt, Tsung?'

'I studied a sketch-map my father once made, Your Honour. I know the way, but I also know that all doors in the corridors leading there are kept securely locked!'

'My assistant will take care of that,' Judge Dee said, rising. 'Mr Kuan won't miss us, let's be on our way!'

'Who knows whether we might not find Mo Mo-te or the one-armed girl in that closed part of the monastery!' Tao Gan said hopefully.

He took the lantern from the corner table, and they went out. Kuan was still snoring peacefully.

13

At this late hour the monastery was deserted. They met no one on the ground floor, or on the stairs leading to the latticed landing over the temple hall.

Judge Dee had a quick look at the passage leading to the store-room but no one was there.

Tsung Lee took them in the opposite direction, through the long passage leading to the tower on the south-west corner, where Sun Ming had his quarters. Arrived in the small hall that gave access to the landing in front of Sun's library, Tsung Lee pulled the narrow door on the right open and went down a flight of stairs. They found themselves in a spacious portal. Pointing to the pair of high, double doors, lavishly decorated with wood carving, the poet whispered:

'That's the entrance to the Gallery of Horrors. That big padlock looks rather formidable!'

'I have seen worse!' Tao Gan grunted. He took a leather folder with various instruments from his capacious sleeve, and set to work. Tsung Lee held the lantern for him.

'I was told that the gallery hadn't been opened for some months,' the judge observed. 'Yet there isn't a speck of dust on the cross-bar!'

'They were in here yesterday, sir,' the poet said. 'A worm-eaten statue had to be repaired.'

'There you are!' Tao Gan said contentedly. He opened the padlock and took the cross-bar down. The judge and Tsung Lee went inside. Tao Gan pulled the door shut behind them. Tsung lifted the lantern high and Judge Dee surveyed the long, broad gallery. It was cold and damp in there. Pulling his robe closer he muttered:

'Disgusting exhibition, as usual!'

'My father used to say that these galleries ought to be abolished, sir,' Tsung remarked.

'He was right!' the judge said caustically.

Tao Gan surveyed the gallery too. He muttered with a sniff:

'All these horrors are no use! People will still get themselves into mischief, horrors disregarding! They are just made that way.'

The wall on their right was covered with scrolls bearing Taoist texts on sin and retribution. But all along the left wall stood a row of life-size statues which represented the torments inflicted on the souls of sinners, in the Taoist Inferno. Here one saw gruesome devils sawing a writhing man in two, there a group of grinning goblins were boiling a man and a woman in an iron kettle. Farther on ox-headed and horse-headed devils were dragging men and women by their hair before the Black Judge of the Nether World, sculptured in relief but with a long beard of real hair. All statues were vividly coloured; the light of Tsung's lantern shone on the leering masks of the demons and the horribly distorted faces of their victims.

The three men walked on quickly, keeping close to the wall on the right so as not to come too near all those horrors. Judge Dee's eye was caught by a woman, stark naked, lying spread-eagled on her back against a large boulder, while a huge blue devil pressed the point of his spear against her breast. Her long hair hung over her face. Her hands and feet had been cut off, and the body of cracked plaster was loaded with heavy chains, but it showed all details with obscene clarity. The next scene was even worse. Two demons, clad like ancient warriors, in blood-stained armour, were hacking a naked man and woman to pieces on a large chopping block, using battle-axes. Of the man only the rump was left, but the woman, lying on her face over the block, was just having her arms cut off.

Quickening his pace Judge Dee said crossly to Tao Gan:

'I'll tell the Abbot to have the statues of those women removed. All these scenes are sufficiently repulsive, they need not include women exposed like that. Such lurid representations are not allowed in an officially recognized place of worship.'

The door at the end of the gallery was not locked. A steep flight of steps brought them to a large, square room.

'Here we must be on the first floor of the north-west tower,' Tsung Lee said. 'If I remember the plan correctly, the door over there gives access to the stairs leading down to the crypt, under the sanctum.'

Tao Gan began to work on the lock.

'This hasn't been opened for a long time,' he remarked. 'It's all rusty.'

It took some time before a snapping sound announced that Tao Gan had sprung the lock. He pushed the heavy door open. A musty odour rose from the darkness below.

Judge Dee took the lantern from Tsung Lee and went carefully down the narrow, uneven steps. When he had counted thirty, the steps made a right turn. He counted again thirty steps, now hewn directly from the rock. He let the light of the lantern fall on the solid iron door that barred his way, fastened by a heavy chain with a padlock. He pressed himself against the damp wall to make room for Tao Gan.

When the gaunt man had also opened this lock and removed the chain, the judge stepped inside. A sound of flapping wings came from the darkness. He quickly drew back. A small black shape fluttered past his head.

'Bats!' he said disgustedly. He went inside and lifted the lantern high above his head. The two others remained standing behind him. Silently they surveyed the awe-inspiring scene.

In the centre of the small, octagonal crypt stood a dais of gilded wood. On it was throned a human figure, sitting in a high abbot's chair of carved red-lacquer. It was dressed in full regalia; a robe of stiff gold brocade with a broad stole of red silk was draped round the narrow shoulders. Under the high tiara, glittering with gold, a brownish, sunken face stared at them with strange eyes that looked like shrivelled slits. A ragged white beard hung from the chin, one strand had become loose. The left hand was hidden under the stole. The other held a long abbot's staff in thin, claw-like fingers.

Judge Dee made a bow. His two companions followed his example.

Then the judge took a step forward and let the light shine on the walls. The stone surface had been polished smooth, and Taoist texts were carved there in beautiful, large characters, filled in with gold lacquer. Against the back wall stood a large box of red leather, secured with a copper padlock. There was no other furniture, but the floor was covered by a thick carpet, showing blue Taoist symbols woven into a gold-brown ground. The air was dry and crisp.

As they were walking round the dais, more small bats flew round the lantern. Judge Dee shooed them away.

'Where could those be coming from?' Tsung Lee asked in a hushed voice.

The judge pointed at two apertures in the ceiling.

'Those are airshafts,' he said. 'Your poem about the two abbots was all wrong, there are no maggots here, it's too dry. You should have said bats.

Judge Dee and his Helpers Inspect the Crypt

127

But probably you couldn't have found a word rhyming with that anyway!'

'Cats!' the poet murmured.

'We are coming to those! The old Abbot painted many of them. Open that box, Tao Gan! It must contain his pictures and manuscripts. I see no other place for storing them.'

Judge Dee and Tsung Lee looked on while Tao Gan sprung the padlock. The box was tightly packed with rolls of paper and silk. Tao Gan unrolled a few from the top. Handing the judge two rolls he said:

'Here are more pictures of that grey cat, Your Honour.'

Judge Dee looked casually at them. One showed the cat playing on the floor with its woollen ball, the other while it was playing in the grass, trying to catch with its raised paw a butterfly. Suddenly he stiffened. He stood stock-still for a while, staring straight ahead of him. Then he put the two pictures back into the box. He said tensely:

'Close the box, I need no further proof! The old Abbot was indeed murdered!'

Tao Gan and Tsung wanted to ask a question, but the judge barked:

'Hurry up with that box, we'll now go and charge the criminal with his foul murder!'

Tao Gan quickly replaced the scrolls, closed the box and ran after the judge. Judge Dee cast one last look at the sunken face of the figure on the dais. Then he bowed, and made for the stairs.

'Aren't the Abbot's quarters in the building over the fourth gate?' he asked Tsung Lee while they were going up.

'Yes, sir! If we go back to the west tower, we can take the passage that leads east, straight to the rooms of the gate-house of the sanctum.'

'You take me there. Tao Gan, you run back through the Gallery of Horrors to the temple, and take the picture of the cat that is hanging above the altar in the side hall. Then you rouse a novice and let him bring you to the Abbot's quarters, along the usual way.'

They completed the climb up to the north-west tower in silence. From there Tao Gan went straight on, Tsung Lee took the judge to the dark passage on their left. Through the shuttered windows they could again hear the wind and rain outside. There were the sounds of earthenware breaking on the flagstones of the central courtyard below.

'The gale is blowing tiles from the roof,' the poet remarked. 'That will be the last of the storm, they usually begin and end with a violent gale.'

The two men came to a halt in front of a solid-looking door. It was locked.

'As far as I remember from the plan, Your Honour,' Tsung Lee said, 'this is the back-door of the Abbot's bedroom.'

Judge Dee rapped hard on it with his knuckles. He pressed his ear to the smooth surface. He thought he heard someone moving about inside. He repeated his knocking. At last there was the sound of a key, and the door was slowly opened a crack. The light of their lantern shone on a haggard face, distorted by fear.

14

When the Abbot recognized the judge he seemed greatly relieved, his tense features relaxed somewhat. He asked haltingly:

'What . . . what gives this person the honour . . .'

'Let's go inside!' Judge Dee interrupted curtly. 'There's an urgent matter I want to talk over with you.'

The Abbot took them through a simply furnished bedroom to the comfortable library adjoining it. Judge Dee noticed at once the queer, cloying smell. It came from a large antique incense-burner, standing on the side table. With a gesture the Abbot invited the judge to sit down in the high-backed armchair next to his desk. He himself went to sit behind it, and motioned Tsung Lee to a chair by the window. He opened his mouth a few times, but apparently he didn't yet trust himself to speak. He evidently had received a bad shock.

The judge leaned back in his armchair. He studied the Abbot's twitching face for a while, then said affably:

'A thousand pardons for disturbing you so late in the night – or so early in the morning, rather! Fortunately I found you still up and about. I see that you are still fully dressed. Did you expect company?'

'No . . . I was taking a brief nap in the armchair in my bedroom,' the Abbot said with a wan smile. 'In a few hours I'll have to conduct the matins, it . . . it didn't seem worth while to change. Why did Your Honour come by the back-door? I thought that . . .'

'You didn't think that the old Abbot had risen from the crypt, did you?' Judge Dee asked quietly. As he saw the sudden panic in True Wisdom's eyes, he added: 'He couldn't, because he is very dead. I can tell you, because I have just come from there.'

The Abbot had now mastered himself. He sat up and asked sharply:

'Why did you go to the crypt? I told you that at this time of the year it – '

'You did,' the judge interrupted him. 'But I felt it necessary to examine the papers left by your predecessor. Now I want to verify a few points about his death, while my memory of what I saw is still fresh. Hence my barging in here at this unusual hour. Let your thoughts go back to that last day of your predecessor's life. You had the noon meal together with him in the refectory. You hadn't seen him during the morning, had you?'

'Only during the matins. Thereafter His Holiness retired to his room, as a matter of fact to this very library. It has always been the private quarters of the abbots of this monastery.'

'I see,' Judge Dee said. He turned round in his chair and looked at the three high windows in the

132

wall behind him. 'Those give on to the central courtyard, I suppose.'

'They do,' the Abbot replied hurriedly. 'During the day this room is very well lighted, that's why my predecessor liked it. Its bright light made it very suitable for painting, the only relaxation he ever indulged in.'

'Very suitable indeed,' the judge remarked. He thought a moment, then went on: 'By the way, when I was talking with you in the reception room, an actor came in, and you commented on their careless behaviour. Did you see who it was before he shut the door again?'

The Abbot, who had succeeded in taking hold of himself, again became ill at ease. He stammered:

'No ... that is to say, yes, I did. It was that swordsman, Mo Mo-te.'

'Thank you.' Judge Dee looked fixedly at the frightened man behind the desk, slowly stroking his long beard.

They sat in silence for a while. Tsung Lee started to shift impatiently in his chair. Judge Dee did not move, he listened to the rain against the shutters. It seemed less heavy than before.

There was a knock on the door. Tao Gan came in with a roll under his arm. After he had handed it to the judge he remained standing by the door.

Judge Dee unrolled the picture and laid it on the desk before his host. He said:

'I gather that this is the last painting Jade Mirror did.'

'Indeed. After the noon meal I had a cup of tea

with him here. Then he dismissed me, saying that he wanted to devote the afternoon to doing a picture of his cat. The poor animal was sitting on that side table of carved ebony over there. I left immediately, as I knew that His Holiness liked to be alone when he worked. The last I saw was that he was spreading a sheet of blank paper out on this desk, and – '

Suddenly the judge got up and hit his fist on the table.

'You are lying!' he barked.

The Abbot shrank back in his chair. He opened his mouth, but the judge shouted:

'Observe this painting, the last work of the great and good man whom you foully murdered by putting the poison of the nightshade in his tea after the noon meal, here in this library!' He quickly bent over the table and pointed at the picture. 'Do you mean to tell me that a man can paint such an intricate picture in the space of one hour? Look at the detailed treatment of the fur, the careful sketch of the carving of the table! It must have taken him at least two hours. You lie when you say that he began to paint it after you had left him. He must have done it in the morning, before the noon meal!'

'Don't dare to say that!' the Abbot said angrily. 'His Holiness was a skilful artist, everybody knows that he worked very quickly. I won't – '

'You can't fool me!' Judge Dee snapped. 'This cat, your victim's pet, did its master its last service! This cat proves clearly that you are lying. Here, look at its eyes! Don't you see that the pupils are wide open? If it had been painted at noontime, in summer, and in this brightly-lit room, the pupils would have been just narrow slits!'

A long shudder shook the Abbot's spare frame. He stared with wide eyes at the picture in front of him. Then he passed his hand over his face. He looked up into the blazing eyes of the judge, and said tonelessly:

'I want to deliver a statement in front of Master Sun Ming.'

'As you like!' Judge Dee replied coldly. He rolled the picture up again and put it in his bosom. The Abbot led them down a broad staircase. Below, he said in the same toneless voice:

'The storm is over. We can go by the courtyard.'

The four men crossed the wet, empty central courtyard, strewn with broken tiles. Judge Dee walked with the Abbot in front, Tao Gan and Tsung Lee following close behind.

The Abbot made for the building west of the temple, and pushed a door open in the corner of the yard. It gave access to a narrow passage that led them straight to the portal in front of the refectory. As they went to the spiral staircase leading up into the south-west tower, a deep voice spoke up:

'What are you people doing here in the deep of night?'

Sun Ming was standing there, carrying a lighted lantern.

Judge Dee said gravely:

'The Abbot wants to make a statement, sir. He expressed the wish to do so in Your Excellency's presence.'

Master Sun lifted the lantern and gave the Abbot an astonished look. He said to him curtly:

'Come up to my library, my friend, we can't engage in delivering statements here in this draughty portal!' Turning to the judge, he asked: 'Is the presence of those two other fellows necessary?'

'I'm afraid it is, sir. They are important witnesses.'

'In that case you had better carry my lantern,' Sun said, handing it to the judge. 'I know my way about.'

He went up the stairs, followed by the Abbot, with Judge Dee, Tao Gan and Tsung close behind him. The judge noticed that his legs felt as if they were made of lead. There seemed to be no end to the winding stairs.

At last they arrived at the top of the dark staircase. Judge Dee lifted his lantern and saw Sun Ming step on to the landing in front of his library. The Abbot followed him. When Judge Dee's head was on a level with the platform, he heard Sun say:

'Mind your step now!' Suddenly he shouted: 'Hold on, man!'

At the same time there was a hoarse cry. Then a sickening thud from the darkness deep below them.

15

Judge Dee stepped hastily on to the landing, holding the lantern high. Sun Ming grabbed his arm, his round face was of a deadly pallor. He said hoarsely:

'The poor fellow groped for the balustrade that wasn't there!'

He let Judge Dee's arm go and wiped the perspiration from his face.

'Run down and have a look!' Judge Dee ordered Tao Gan. And, to Sun Ming: 'He won't have survived that fall. Let's go inside, sir.'

The two men entered the library. Tsung Lee had followed Tao Gan downstairs.

'The poor wretch!' Sun said as he sat down behind his desk. 'What was it all about, Dee?'

Judge Dee took the chair opposite, his legs were trembling from fatigue. He took the rolled-up picture from his bosom and placed it on the desk. Then he spoke:

'I paid a visit to the crypt, sir, and there looked at a few pictures the old Abbot Jade Mirror made of his cat. It struck me that he used to do those in great detail. On one painting the cat's pupils were just slits, it must have been done at noon. Then I remembered that on his last picture, which you showed me in the temple, the pupils of the cat were wide open. That proved to me that the picture was painted in the morning, and not at noon, as True Wisdom had always said.'

He unrolled the scroll and pointed to the cat's eyes.

'I can't understand what you are getting at, Dee!' Sun said annoyed. 'What has all this to do with Jade Mirror's death? I was there myself, I tell you, the man died peacefully and – '

'Allow me to explain, sir,' Judge Dee interrupted respectfully. He then told Sun about the reference to nightshades in the old Abbot's letter to Dr Tsung, and how the symptoms of nightshade poisoning accorded well with the old Abbot's behaviour during his last hours. He added diffidently: 'If I may say so, sir, it has often struck me that Taoist texts are always couched in a highly obscure and ambiguous language. One could imagine that the old Abbot's last sermon was in fact a confused mixture of various religious passages he remembered. It needed the commentary of the Chief Abbot to make sense. I presume he chose some mystic terms from the Abbot's sermon, and made those the theme for a lucid discussion, or he . . .' He broke off, giving Master Sun an anxious look.

But Sun was perplexed, he made no attempt to speak up in favour of Taoist texts. He just sat there, slowly shaking his large head. The judge went on:

'True Wisdom put a large dose of the poison in Jade Mirror's tea when, after the noon meal, they were having a cup together in the library. The picture was nearly finished then. The Abbot had spent the entire morning on it, first doing the cat itself, then painting in background and details. He had only to do the bamboo leaves when he interrupted his work for the noon meal. After he had drunk the poisoned tea, True Wisdom left and told the two monks who were waiting outside that the Abbot should not be disturbed, because he was starting on a picture. The poison soon brought him into a state of mental excitement, he started to hum Taoist hymns, then began to talk to himself. There can be no doubt that he thought he was becoming inspired. It didn't enter his mind that he had been poisoned. You'll remember, sir, that he did not say one word about that being his last sermon, nor about his wanting to depart from this world after he would have finished. There was no reason to. He only wanted to pass on to his followers the revelation that Heaven had granted him. Thereafter he leaned back in his chair, wanting to rest awhile after his lengthy speech. But then he passed away – a happy man.'

'Almighty Heaven!' Sun now exclaimed. 'You must be right, Dee! But why did the fool murder Jade Mirror? And why did he insist on making his confession in front of me?'

'I think,' Judge Dee replied, 'that True Wisdom had committed a sordid crime, and that he feared that the old Abbot had discovered it and was planning to expose him. Jade Mirror wrote in his last letter to Dr Tsung that he suspected that immoral acts were being committed with the girls who came to stay here to be initiated and to be ordained as nuns. If this had come out, True Wisdom would of course have been finished.'

Sun passed his hand over his eyes in a weary gesture.

'Immoral acts!' he muttered. 'The fool must have been dabbling in black magic, involving rites with woman partners. August Heaven, I am responsible also, Dee! I shouldn't have kept myself shut up in my library all the time; I should have kept an eye on what was going on. And Jade Mirror is guilty too, in a way. Why didn't he at once tell me about his suspicions? I hadn't the faintest idea that . . .'

His voice trailed off. Judge Dee resumed:

'I think that True Wisdom, together with a villain who now calls himself Mo Mo-te, was responsible for the fate of the three girls who died here last year. They must have been forced to take part in the unspeakable secret rites, just as those others who came here before the old Abbot died. Mo Mo-te has now revisited this monastery, in the guise of a member of Kuan's troupe. Mo probably threatened the Abbot and tried to blackmail him; I noticed that the Abbot was afraid of Mo. That, together with broad hints at the old Abbot having been murdered with the poison of the nightshade, made in public by Tsung Lee, must have made True Wisdom desperate. When, at the end of the banquet, he saw Tsung Lee talking with me, and when directly thereafter I told True Wisdom that I wanted to visit the crypt, he thought I was planning to institute an investigation. He became frantic, and tried to kill me. He dealt me a blow on my head from behind, but before I lost consciousness I had perceived the smell of a peculiar incense he burns in the bedroom. Ordinarily one doesn't smell it when one is near him, but I got a waft of it from the folds of his robe when he lifted his arm to hit me. Later he spied on me when I was talking with my assistant, and when he fled I again noticed that particular smell. The man must have lost his head completely.'

Sun Ming nodded forlornly. After a while he asked:

'But why did the fellow insist on delivering a statement in front of me? If he had thought I would speak up in his favour, he must have been an even greater fool than I had always thought he was!'

'Before I answer that question, sir,' Judge Dee said, 'I would like to ask you first whether True Wisdom was aware of the fact that the balustrade of the landing was broken?'

'Of course he was!' Sun replied. 'I told him myself that I wanted to have it repaired. He was diligent enough, I must grant him that!'

'In that case,' Judge Dee said gravely, 'he committed suicide.'

'Nonsense! I myself saw him groping for that balustrade, Dee!'

'He fooled both you and me,' the judge said. 'Remember that he couldn't have known that we would meet you at the bottom of the staircase leading up here. He thought that you would be in your library. He never intended to meet you, sir, let alone make a statement. He only wanted to come up here because he knew he was lost, and because the landing was the best place he could think of for committing suicide before I could arrest him. He pretended it was an accident in order to safeguard his reputation and the interests of his family. For now we shall never be able to say with absolute certainty what part he took in all that happened here. Your unexpected appearance did not materially change his scheme.'

Tao Gan and Tsung Lee came in.

'He broke his neck, Your Honour,' the former announced soberly. 'He must have died instantly. I fetched the Prior, they are now bringing the corpse to the side hall of the temple, to lie in state there pending the official burial. I explained that it had been an accident.' Turning to Sun he added: 'The Prior wishes to speak to you, sir.'

Judge Dee rose. He said to Sun:

'For the time being we'd better keep to that theory of an accident. Perhaps Your Excellency will be so kind as to discuss with the Prior the necessary measures to be taken. I suppose the Chief Abbot in the capital must be informed as soon as possible!'

'We'll send a messenger first thing tomorrow morning,' Sun said. 'We'll also have to ascertain the wishes of His Holiness regarding the succession. Pending his answer, the Prior can take

care of the routine administration of this monastery.'

'I hope that tomorrow morning you'll kindly
help me to draw up the official report about this,
sir,' the judge said. 'I'll leave the picture of the cat
here, it's an important piece of evidence.'

Sun Ming nodded. He gave the judge an
appraising look, then said:

'You had better go and get a few hours' sleep,
Dee! You look a bit off colour!'

'I still have to arrest Mo, sir!' the judge replied
dejectedly. 'I am convinced that Mo is the real
criminal, more guilty than the Abbot. It must
depend on Mo's testimony whether we report the
Abbot's death just now as suicide, or as death by
misadventure. And, now that the Abbot is dead,
Mo is the only one who can tell us what really
happened to the three girls who died here.'

'What does the fellow look like?' Sun asked.
'You say he is an actor? I watched the entire
mystery play, except for the last scene.'

'Mo was on the stage all the time, he acted the
part of the Spirit of Death. But you couldn't see
his face, sir, because he wore one of those large
wooden masks. I saw him in the last scene, where
he performed a sword-dance, but then his face
was painted. I suspect that now he is posing as one
of the monks here. He is a tall, broad-shouldered
fellow, and usually looks rather morose.'

'Most of the monks do,' Sun muttered. 'Wrong
diet, I suppose. How do you expect to find him,
Dee?'

143

'That is what I must try to work out now, sir!' Judge Dee replied with a rueful smile. 'I can't settle this case without Mo's full confession.'

He took his leave with a deep bow. As he went to the door, with Tao Gan and Tsung Lee, the small Prior came in, looking more nervous than ever.

16

When the three men entered the temple hall they found the almoner, talking in a hushed voice to a small group of monks. Seeing Judge Dee he came quickly forward and led him silently to the side hall.

The Abbot's corpse had been laid on a high bier and covered with a piece of red brocade, embroidered in gold thread with Taoist symbols. The judge lifted one end. He looked for a while at the dead man's still face. As he let it drop again, the almoner whispered:

'Four monks will be here all night reading prayers, Your Honour. The Prior plans to announce the Abbot's demise in a few hours, during matins.'

Judge Dee expressed his condolence, then went back to the front hall, where Tao Gan and Tsung Lee stood waiting for him. The poet asked diffidently:

'May I invite Your Honour to have a cup of tea up in my room?'

'I refuse to climb any more steps!' Judge Dee replied firmly. 'Tell one of those monks to bring a large pot of bitter tea to that room over there!'

He went to the small cabinet over on the other side of the front hall. It was apparently used as a reception room. Judge Dee sat down at the tea-table, a beautiful antique piece of carved sandal-wood. He motioned Tao Gan to take the chair opposite him. Silently the judge studied the painted portraits of Taoist Immortals, yellowed by age, that were suspended in gorgeous frames on the walls. Through the open-work carving in the wall above them he could vaguely see the heads of the large gilded statues on the altar in the dim temple hall.

Tsung Lee came in carrying a large teapot. He poured out three cups. The judge told him to be seated also.

While sipping their tea they listened to the monotonous chant that came drifting over to them from the side hall opposite. The monks by the Abbot's bier had started intoning the prayers for the dead.

Judge Dee sat motionless, slumped back in his chair. He felt completely exhausted. His legs and his back were throbbing with a dull ache, and he had a queer, empty feeling in his head. He tried to review the circumstances that led up to the old Abbot's murder and True Wisdom's suicide. He had a vague feeling that some features still needed further explanation; that there were some isolated facts which would complete his mental picture of Mo Mo-te – if only he could find the correct interpretation. But his brain was numb, he couldn't think clearly. Mo Mo-te's helmet kept appearing before him. He had the distinct feeling that there was something wrong with that helmet. His thoughts became confused, he suddenly realized that the monotonous chant of the monks was lulling him to sleep.

He suppressed a yawn and sat up with an effort. Placing his elbows on the table he looked at his two companions. Tao Gan's thin face was as impassive as ever. Tsung Lee looked utterly tired, his face was sagging. The judge reflected that, now that the poet's fatigue had made him drop his habitual insolent airs, he really wasn't an unprepossessing youngster. Judge Dee emptied his teacup, then addressed him:

'Now that you have executed your late father's command, Tsung Lee, you'd better settle down to a serious study of the Confucianist classics, so as to prepare yourself for the literary examinations. You may yet prove yourself a worthy son of your distinguished father!' He gave the youngster a sour look, then he pushed his cap back from his forehead, and continued in a brisk voice: 'We must now have a consultation about how we can catch Mo Mo-te, and save his most recent victim. He must tell us where he concealed that one-armed woman, and who she is.'

'A one-armed woman?' Tsung Lee asked astonished.

'Yes,' Judge Dee said, giving him a sharp look. 'Ever seen such a mutilated woman about here?'

Tsung Lee shook his head.

'No, sir, I have been here now more than two weeks, but I never even heard about a one-armed woman. Unless,' he added with a smile, 'Your

Honour would be referring to that statue in the Gallery of Horrors!'

'A statue?' Judge Dee asked. It was now his turn to be astonished.

'Yes, the one with all those chains, sir. Its left arm had become worm-eaten, and it fell off. They repaired it very quickly though, I must say.' As Judge Dee looked fixedly at him he added: 'You know, that naked woman being speared by a blue devil. I heard you remark to Tao Gan that you – '

Judge Dee hit his fist on the table.

'You utter fool!' he burst out. 'Why didn't you tell me that earlier?'

'I thought . . . I told you about a statue being repaired, when we entered the gallery, sir. And . . .'

The judge had jumped up and grabbed the lantern.

'Come along quick, you two!' he barked and ran out into the temple hall.

He seemed to have forgotten his fatigue completely. He rushed up the stairs two at a time to the landing above the temple. Tao Gan and Tsung Lee had difficulty in keeping up with him.

Panting, the judge took them through the west passage to the tower, then ran down the steps that led to the entrance of the Gallery of Horrors. He kicked the door open and went inside. He halted in front of the blue devil and the naked woman, spread-eagled against the boulder.

'Look, she is bleeding!' he muttered.

Tao Gan and Tsung Lee stared aghast at the thin stream of blood that trickled along the crusted paint on the woman's breast from the spot where the spear-point had entered.

Judge Dee bent and carefully brushed aside the hair that covered the face.

'White Rose!' Tsung Lee gasped. 'They've killed her!'

'No,' Judge Dee said. 'See, her fingers are twitching.'

The body had been covered with a thin coat of whitewash, but the hands and feet had been painted black. A casual observer would not see them against the dark background.

The girl's eyelids fluttered. She gave them one glance from eyes half-crazed with pain and fear, then the bluish lids came down again. A strap of leather ran over the lower half of her face. While gagging her effectively, at the same time it kept her head fixed tightly to the wall.

Tsung Lee stretched out his hands to remove the gag, but the judge pushed him back roughly.

'Keep your hands off!' he ordered. 'You might hurt her worse than she already is! Leave this to us!'

Tao Gan had taken off the chains that were wound round her waist, arms and legs. He said:

'This ironware serves only to conceal the clamps that fix her limbs, sir!' He pointed to iron hooks round her ankles, thighs and upper and lower arms. Then he quickly took from his sleeve his folder of instruments.

'Wait!' Judge Dee ordered.

He had closely examined the spear-point. Now

he carefully pressed down the flesh surrounding it till the point came free. Blood welled up and stained the coat of white paint that covered the girl's body. It didn't seem more than a flesh-wound. With his strong hands the judge bent the spear so that it pointed away from the girl's body, then broke the shaft with a quick twist. The hand of the wooden devil cracked and fell to the floor.

'Now you go ahead with the legs!' he snapped at Tao Gan. 'Give me a pair of pincers!'

While Tao Gan began to loosen the iron clamps that secured the girl's legs, the judge set to work on the gag. When he had pulled out the nails that fixed the ends of the leather strap to the wall, he removed the wad of cotton wool from the girl's mouth, then started with infinite care on the clamps that had cut deep into the flesh of her arms.

'Expert workmanship!' Tao Gan muttered with grudging admiration. He was loosening the clamp that held her right thigh.

Tsung Lee had buried his face in his hands. He was sobbing convulsively. The judge barked at him:

'Hey there! Support her head and shoulders!'

As Tsung Lee put his arm round her shoulders and held her limp body upright, Judge Dee helped Tao Gan to remove the last clamp that held her right arm. The three men lifted her from the boulder and laid her on the floormats. The judge took off his neckcloth and wrapped it around her waist. Tsung Lee squatted at her side, stroking her cheeks and whispering endearing words. But the girl was in a dead faint.

Judge Dee and Tao Gan wrenched two long spears from the hands of a pair of green devils farther on. They laid the spears side by side on the floor. Tao Gan took off his upper robe and fastened it to the shafts so as to make a primitive stretcher. When they had laid the girl on it, Tao Gan and Tsung Lee took hold of the ends of the shafts.

'Take her to Miss Ting's room!' Judge Dee ordered.

17

Judge Dee had to knock for a long time before Miss Ting opened. She wore only a thin bed-robe. Looking the judge up and down with sleep-heavy eyes, she said:

'You could be my husband, using my room at all hours!'

'Shut up and get out of the way!' the judge said crossly. She stepped back and looked, dumb-founded, at the two men as they carried their burden inside. While they were putting the uncon-scious girl on Miss Ting's bed, Judge Dee said to her:

'Fan the coals in that brazier and heat up this room. Prepare a large pot of hot tea and make her drink as much as possible. She was exposed naked for many hours in a cold and damp gallery, and she may have got a dangerous chill. Also, although the paint is only ordinary whitewash as far as I can see, it may have affected the skin. You should remove it quickly with a towel soaked in hot water. Be careful, the wound on her breast is only superficial, but the bruises on her arms and legs may be worse than they seem. Verify also whether her back is injured. As an acrobat you know all about sprained muscles and bone-setting, don't you?'

Miss Ting nodded. She cast a pitying glance at the still figure on the bed.

'I'll get some drugs and plasters now,' the judge added. 'These two men will stand guard outside the door. Set to work!'

Miss Ting asked no questions but immediately began to revive the coals in the brazier with a bamboo fan. Judge Dee took Tao Gan and Tsung Lee outside. He said:

'Fetch Mr Kang. If Mo should appear, arrest him. Not too gently!'

He rushed upstairs, to his own quarters on the third floor.

He roused the sleeping maids. When they had opened the door he went into the bedroom, lighted only by two burned-down candles. Through the open bed curtains he saw that his three wives were sleeping peacefully lying close together under the embroidered quilt.

He tiptoed to their medicine chest and rummaged about in its drawers till he had found the box with the oil-plasters and a few small boxes with salves and powders. As he turned round he saw that his First Lady had awakened. She raised herself to a sitting position. Pulling her night-robe up to cover her bare torso she looked at him with sleep-heavy eyes.

Judge Dee gave her a reassuring smile, then went out again.

Back in front of Miss Ting's room, Tao Gan reported that Kang I-te's room was empty, neither he nor his bear was there. They had seen no one.

'Go to Mrs Pao's room,' the judge ordered, 'and bring her here.'

'Who was the fiend who tortured her, Your Honour?' Tsung Lee asked tensely. His face was distorted with anger and anxiety.

'We'll know soon!' the judge answered curtly.

Tao Gan came back. The door of Mrs Pao's room had been locked. He had forced it open but nobody was there. He had found only a bundle of clothes belonging to White Rose. Mrs Pao's luggage was missing, and neither of the two beds had been slept in.

Judge Dee made no comment. He started pacing up and down the corridor, his hands behind his back.

After a long wait Miss Ting opened the door and beckoned the judge.

'I'll call you when I am ready,' he said to the two men, and followed her inside.

He walked up to the bed. Miss Ting folded the covers back. While she held the candle close Judge Dee examined the bruises on the white body. The girl was still unconscious but her lips twitched when the judge probed the deep cuts left by the clamps.

He righted himself and took a small box from his sleeve.

'Dissolve the contents in a cup of hot tea,' he ordered. 'It's a pain-stilling soporific.'

Then he further examined the girl's body. He didn't like the heart-beat, but there seemed to be no internal lesions. She was a virgin, and there

154

were no signs that she had been beaten except for a bluish spot on her left temple. He put salve on the bruises, then covered them with thick oil-plasters. He saw to his satisfaction that Miss Ting had pasted the membrane of an egg over the wound on her breast. The judge covered her up again. He took a pinch of white powder from another box he had brought and inserted it in White Rose's nostrils.

Miss Ting handed him the cup with the medicine. On a sign from the judge she raised the girl's head. The girl sneezed and opened her eyes. The judge made her drink the medicine, then let her lie back again. He sat down on the edge of the bed. The girl stared up at him with wide, uncomprehending eyes.

'Call the two men here!' Judge Dee ordered Miss Ting. 'Soon she'll be able to talk, and I want them to be present as witnesses.'

'Her condition isn't . . . dangerous?' Miss Ting asked anxiously.

'Not too bad,' Judge Dee said. Giving her a quick smile he patted her on the shoulder and added: 'You did very well. Now get those two fellows!'

As Tao Gan and Tsung Lee came in, the judge said softly to White Rose:

'You are safe now, my dear. Presently you'll have a nice long sleep.'

He didn't like the queer stare in the girl's eyes. 'You talk to her!' he ordered Tsung Lee.

The poet bent over her and softly called her

name. Suddenly the girl seemed to understand. She looked at him and asked in a barely audible voice:

'What happened? Did I have a nightmare?'

Judge Dee made a peremptory sign to Tsung. The poet knelt down by the side of the bedstead and took the girl's hand in his, stroking it softly. The judge said to the girl reassuringly:

'Whatever it was, it's all past and done with now!'

'But I still see it all before me!' she cried out. 'All those horrible faces!'

'Tell me about it!' Judge Dee said encouragingly. 'You know how it is with bad dreams, don't you? Once you have told them they lose their power over you, and they are gone, gone for ever. Who took you up to the gallery?'

White Rose heaved a deep sigh. Staring at the curtains above her she said slowly:

'I remember that after watching the stage show I felt very confused. I have always been close to my brother. I had been terribly frightened when that man threatened him with his sword. I muttered some excuse to Mrs Pao, and joined my brother backstage. I told him that I was in awful difficulties, and that I wanted to talk with him alone. He told me to go up to his room, posing as him. He had disguised himself as an actress, you know.'

She gave the judge a questioning look.

'Yes, I know all about that,' Judge Dee said.

A Young Girl in the Hands of Evil Persons

157

'What happened after you met us up in the corridor?'

'When I had rounded the corner I ran into Mrs Pao. She was very angry, she cursed me soundly and practically dragged me to our room. There she made some excuses, she said she was responsible for me, and couldn't allow me to associate with an actress of dubious reputation. I was angry because of her brusque behaviour, and that gave me the courage to tell her that I wasn't sure that I wanted to become a nun after all. I added that I wanted to talk things over with Miss Ou-yang, whom I said I had known well in the capital.

'Mrs Pao took this information rather calmly. She said that the decision was of course up to me. But that the monastery would have started preparations for my initiation, and that she would have to inform the Abbot immediately. When she came back, she told me that the Abbot wanted to see me.'

Turning her eyes to Tsung Lee she continued:

'Mrs Pao took me over to the temple. We went up the staircase on the right. After having gone up and down a few flights of steps we entered a small dressing-room. Mrs Pao said I would have to change into a nun's cowl, as that was the proper dress in which to be received by the Abbot. I suddenly realized that they were going to try to force me to become a nun. I refused.

'Then Mrs Pao flew into a rage. I didn't recognize her any more, she called me awful names. She tore my clothes off. I was so stupefied by the

158

unbelievable change in her that I hardly resisted. She pushed me naked into the next room.'

She gave the judge a pitiable look. He quickly made her drink another cup of tea. She went on in a low voice:

'I saw a large, luxuriously appointed bedroom. A couch stood against the back wall, the yellow brocade curtains were half drawn. A muffled voice spoke from there: "Come here, my bride, you shall now be properly initiated!" I knew at once that I had fallen into a trap set by evil people, and that I must try to escape. I turned round to the door, but the woman grabbed me and quickly bound my hands behind my back. Then she started dragging me by my hair to the couch. I kicked her and screamed for help as loud as I could. "Leave her!" the voice said. "I want to have a good look at her!" Mrs Pao forced me down on my knees in front of the couch, then stepped back. I heard a chuckle from the bedstead. It sounded so horrible that I burst out crying. "That's better!" Mrs Pao said. "Now be a good girl and do as he says!" I shouted at her that they would have to kill me first. "Shall I get the whip?" the loathsome woman asked. But the voice said: "No, it wouldn't do to break that nice skin. She needs a little time, to reflect. Put her to sleep!" Mrs Pao stepped up to me and hit me a sharp blow on the side of my head. I fainted.'

Tsung Lee wanted to say something, but Judge Dee raised his hand. After a brief pause White Rose went on:

'An excruciating pain in my back made me regain my senses. I was half lying, half hanging over some hard thing, I couldn't see well because my hair was hanging over my face. I tried to open my mouth but I had been gagged. My arms and legs were held by clamps that cut into my flesh at the slightest attempt to move. My back was aching and my skin taut all over, as if it was covered with a thin crust of something.

'I felt terrible, but I forgot all pain when I saw through the hair a horrible blue face leering at me. I thought I had died and that I was in the Nether World; I fainted from sheer terror. It was again the pain in my arms and legs that made me come to. By breathing hard through my nose I could blow the hairs apart a little, and I realized that the devil pressing the spear to my breast was in fact a wooden statue. I understood that I had been made to replace one of the statues in the Gallery of Horrors and that my body had been covered with a thin coat of paint. My relief at still being alive was soon replaced by a new terror. Someone must be standing behind me with a candle. What new torture were they planning for me, lying there completely defenceless? Then the light went out. All was pitch-dark. I heard the sound of soft footsteps, moving away. I made a frantic attempt to open my mouth; anything was better than being left lying there alone in the dark. Soon the silence was broken by the sound of rats scurrying about . . .'

She closed her eyes, a long shiver shook her

body. Tsung Lee started to cry, his tears dropped on her hand. She looked up and continued wearily to the judge:

'I don't know how long I was there, I was half crazed by pain and fear, and the damp cold seemed to penetrate to my very bones. At last I saw a light and heard voices. I recognized yours, sir, and did my utmost to give you a sign. I tried to move my feet and my fingers, but they were completely numb. I heard you make a remark on my unseemly exposure, but ... but I did have a loincloth, at least, didn't I?'

She gave him an embarrassed look.

'Certainly!' Judge Dee replied quickly. 'The other statues hadn't, though. Hence my remark.'

'I thought so!' she said relieved. 'But I didn't know for certain, because of the layer of paint, you see. Well, then ... then you went on.'

'I knew my only hope was to draw your attention when you would pass again on your way back. I forced myself to think clearly. Suddenly it came to me that, if I could move my breast in such a way that the spear-point resting against it would cut into my flesh, the blood would show clearly on the white paint and thus might catch your eye. With a supreme effort I succeeded in moving my torso a little. The pain of the spear entering my flesh was nothing compared to the agonizing pain in my back and arms. The crusted paint prevented me from feeling whether much blood had come out. But then I heard a drop fall on the floor. I knew I had succeeded, and that gave me courage.

161

'Soon I heard footsteps again. Someone came running through the gallery; he rushed past me without another look. I knew that you would come too, but it took a very long time, it seemed. At last you came . . .'

'You are a very brave girl,' Judge Dee said. 'I have only two questions to ask you, then you must have a rest. You gave a general description of how Mrs Pao took you to the room where that man was waiting for you. Couldn't you supply me with some more details about the way you went?'

White Rose frowned in an effort to remember.

'I am certain,' she said, 'that it was in one of the buildings east of the temple. But as to the rest . . . I had never been there before, and we made so many turns . . .'

'Did you pass, perhaps, a square landing with a screen of lattice-work all around it?'

She shook her head forlornly.

'I really don't remember!' she replied.

'It doesn't matter. Tell me only whether you recognized the voice that came from the bedstead. Could it have been the Abbot?'

Again she shook her head.

'I still hear that hateful voice in my ears, but it doesn't remind me of anyone I know. And I have good ears.' She added with a faint smile: 'I recognized Tsung Lee's voice when you entered the gallery the first time, though I only heard it in the distance. The relief when . . .'

'It was Tsung Lee who gave me the idea that you

were in the gallery,' Judge Dee remarked. 'Without him I wouldn't have found you.'

She turned her head and looked affectionately at the kneeling youngster. Then she lifted her head to the judge and said weakly:

'I feel so peaceful and happy now! I can never repay you for . . .'

'You can!' Judge Dee said dryly. 'Teach this fellow to make better poetry!'

As he rose the girl smiled faintly. Her eyelids fluttered, the sleeping-drug was taking effect. Turning to Miss Ting, the judge whispered:

'As soon as she is asleep, you throw that youngster out and rub her gently all over with this ointment here.'

There was a knock on the door. Kang I-te came in, dressed as a man.

'I have just put my bear outside,' he said. 'What is all this commotion?'

'Ask Miss Ting!' the judge said gruffly. 'I have other things to do.' He beckoned Tao Gan to follow him.

Miss Ting had been staring at Kang with wide eyes. Now she gasped:

'You are a man!'

'That ought to solve your problem,' Judge Dee remarked to her. Kang had eyes only for her, he had hardly noticed the poet and the still figure on the bed. The last Judge Dee saw him do was clasp Miss Ting in his arms.

18

Outside the judge said sourly to Tao Gan:

'I'd better resign as magistrate and set up business as a professional matchmaker. I have brought together two young couples, but I can't find a dangerous maniac! Let's go to your room, we must devise a plan, and quick!'

While they were walking down the corridor, Tao Gan said sadly:

'I am awfully sorry, sir, that, when passing through the gallery to fetch the painting from the temple, I didn't pause to have a second look at that poor naked woman. Then I would have noticed the blood and . . .'

'You needn't be sorry,' the judge remarked dryly. 'It does you credit. Leave it to your colleague Ma Joong to gape at unclothed women!'

Seated in Tao Gan's small room, Judge Dee silently drank the tea his lieutenant made for him. Then he sighed and said:

'Well, I know now that it was the armless wooden statue from the Gallery of Horrors that I saw Mo move about in that secret hide-out of his. So we have found the one-armed woman, but I still can't understand how I could have seen the original wooden statue through a window that isn't there! However, let's leave that problem for the time being, and concentrate on the new, concrete facts we learned. Mo must have used Mrs Pao as a procuress, and the dead Abbot must have connived at their sordid affairs. Mo must have planned to place Miss Kang in the Gallery of Horrors for some time. He had removed the wooden statue before we arrived here, and probably also prepared the clamps in the wall. The cheek of that villain to go on with his infernal scheme right under my nose!' The judge tugged angrily at his beard. 'When Mrs Pao had informed Mo and the Abbot that White Rose was thinking of giving up her plan of becoming a nun, and wanted to establish contact with Miss Ou-yang, they decided to act quickly. They knew I was scheduled to leave the monastery this morning, and if I should inquire after her they could easily explain the girl's absence by saying that she had gone into retreat for a few days in the forbidden part of the monastery. Thereafter they would have cowed the poor girl so thoroughly by their infernal tortures that she wouldn't have dared to denounce them, and they would doubtless have found some way to explain things to Miss Ou-yang, or Kang I-te rather, and to Tsung Lee. By then she would have been raped, and she herself wouldn't have liked to see her brother or the poet again. Those unspeakable fiends!'

He knitted his thick eyebrows. Tao Gan quietly pulled at the three long hairs on his cheek. No human depravity could ever astonish him. The judge resumed:

'The Abbot escaped earthly justice, but we'll get Mo Mo-te, and he is the main criminal. I don't think the Abbot had the pluck; he was a coward at heart. But Mo is a completely ruthless, perverted maniac. There's no time for half-measures now, Tao Gan! I'll go and rouse Master Sun. We'll have all the inmates assembled in the large hall and we'll let Kuan Lai and Kang I-te look them over. If Mo isn't found among them, we'll search the entire accursed place, as I had already planned.'

Tao Gan looked doubtful.

'I am afraid, sir, that we can't have the whole monastery roused without Mo suspecting that the commotion has something to do with him. He would have fled before the check was afoot. The storm is over, and Heaven knows how many exits this place has. Once he was in the mountains it would prove very difficult to catch him. It would be quite different, of course, if we had Ma Joong, Chiao Tai, and the rest of the staff here, with twenty constables or so. But with only the two of us . . .' He didn't complete the sentence.

Judge Dee nodded unhappily. He had to agree that his lieutenant was right. But what to do then? Absentmindedly he took up a chopstick, and tried to balance the saucer of his teacup on its tip.

'It's a great pity that we haven't a plan of this monastery,' Tao Gan resumed. 'If we had one, we could probably make a good guess where that bedroom to which Mrs Pao took White Rose is. It can't be far from the store-room where Your Honour saw Mo putting away the wooden statue

166

of the naked woman from the gallery. And then we could also verify the thickness of the walls there.'

'Master Sun showed me a diagram,' Judge Dee said. 'A kind of outline of the plan the monastery is built on.' He kept his eyes on the saucer; he thought he had got it nearly balanced. 'That was a great help for my general orientation. But of course it didn't give any details.'

He let the saucer go and lifted the chopstick at the same time. The saucer fell and broke into pieces on the stone floor.

Tao Gan stooped and picked the broken pieces up. Trying to fit them together on the table, he asked curiously:

'What were you trying to do, sir?'

'Oh,' the judge replied a little self-consciously, 'it's a trick Miss Ting did. You make the saucer whirl round on top of the chopstick, you see. It can't fly away because of the rim round the bottom. It's quite a neat trick. That whirling saucer reminded me of the round Taoist symbol Master Sun drew at the top of his diagram, the two primordial forces turning round and round in eternal interaction. Funny I let it drop. When I saw Miss Ting doing it, it looked very easy!'

'Most tricks look easy when they are done well!' Tao Gan remarked with his thin smile. 'But as a matter of fact they ask for very long practice! Good, there's no piece missing. Tomorrow I'll mend this saucer, then it can still be used for many more years!'

'What made you so parsimonious, Tao Gan?' Judge Dee asked curiously. 'I know that you have ample means, and no family obligations. You needn't become a wastrel, even if you don't grudge every single copper!'

His thin lieutenant gave him a shy look. He said, rather diffidently:

'Heaven has presented us with so many good things, sir, and gratis too! A roof to shelter us, food for our stomach, clothes for our body. I am always afraid that some day Heaven'll become angry, seeing that we take all those good things for granted, even spend them recklessly. Therefore I can't bear to throw away anything that can still be used in some way or another. Look, sir, there'll only remain that one bad crack, the one that cuts horizontally through the flower design. But that can't be helped!'

Judge Dee sat up in his chair. He stared fixedly at the reassembled saucer that Tao Gan held together in his cupped hands.

Suddenly he jumped up and started to walk back and forth in the small room, muttering to himself. Tao Gan looked up, then stared again at the broken saucer in his hands. He wondered what the judge had seen there.

Judge Dee halted in front of Tao Gan. He exclaimed excitedly:

'I am a fool, Tao Gan! I have let myself be led around by my nose, that's what I've done! There's no need to assemble all the inmates, I know where to find our man! Come along, I'll go to Master

Sun's library. You'll wait for me on the landing over the temple!'

He took the lantern and ran out, followed by Tao Gan.

The two men went down. They parted in the empty courtyard.

Judge Dee crossed over to the west wing, passed through the portal of the refectory, and ascended the stairs to Sun's quarters.

He knocked several times on the carved door, but there was no answer. He pushed, and found that the door wasn't locked. He went inside.

The library was in semi-darkness, the candles burning low. The judge went over to the narrow door behind the desk, which presumably led to Sun's bedroom. He knocked again. He pressed his ear against the door, but heard nothing. He tried to open it, but it was securely locked.

He turned round and pensively surveyed the room. Then he stepped up to the scroll with the diagram, and looked for a while intently at the round symbol of the two forces depicted at the top. He turned to the door and left. Giving the broken balustrade a brief look, he entered the passage leading east to the square landing over the temple hall.

The judge vaguely heard the murmur of prayers coming up from the temple-nave below. Tao Gan was nowhere to be seen. He shrugged his shoulders and took the corridor leading to the store-room. Its door was standing ajar.

He went inside and lifted his lantern high. The

room was exactly as he had seen it the last time he was there looking for Mo Mo-te. But the double door of the antique cupboard in the farthest corner was standing open. He ran up to it, stepped inside and held his lantern close to the picture of the two dragons on the back wall. The round circle in between them was indeed the Taoist symbol of the two forces, but the dividing line was horizontal. When he had asked Sun about it he had forgotten that it had been here that he had seen the circle thus divided. Tao Gan's remarks and the broken saucer had made him see the connexion.

He now also saw what he hadn't noticed before, namely that there was a small dot in each half of the circle, the germ mentioned by Sun when he had explained the meaning of the symbol to him. Looking closer, the dots turned out to be in fact small holes, bored deeply into the wood. He tapped the circle with his knuckle. No, it wasn't wood, it was an iron disk. And a narrow groove separated it from the lacquered surface surrounding it.

He thought he knew what those two holes in a round metal disk meant. He lifted his cap and pulled the hair-needle from his top-knot. Inserting its point into one of the holes, he tried to make the disk turn to the left. It didn't budge. Then he tried the opposite direction, holding the hair-needle with two hands. Now the disk turned round. He could make it turn easily five times, then it seemed to get stuck. With some difficulty he succeeded in making it turn round four more times. The right half of the back wall of the cup-board started to move a little, like a door about to swing open. He heard vague sounds on the other side. He softly pushed the door shut again.

He stepped back into the room, ran out into the corridor and looked around on the landing. Tao Gan hadn't come yet. Well, he would have to do without a witness. He went back to the store-room, entered the cupboard, and pulled the door open.

He saw a narrow passage only three feet wide, running five feet or so to the right, parallel with the wall. With two quick strides he had turned the corner. He looked into a small room, dimly lit by only one dust-covered oil-lamp hanging from the low ceiling. A tall, broad-backed man stood bent over the bamboo couch that took up the back wall, rubbing it with a piece of cloth. On the floor the judge saw a kitchen chopper lying in a pool of blood.

19

The man righted himself and turned round. Seeing the judge standing there, he said with a benign smile:

'So you found this secret room all by yourself! You are a clever fellow, Dee! Sit down and tell me how you did it! You can sit here on the couch, I've just cleaned it. But mind the blood on the floor!'

Judge Dee looked quickly at the life-size wooden statue of a naked woman that was standing in the corner. The plaster was peeling off, and where the left arm should have been there was only a ragged stump of worm-eaten wood. He sat down by the other's side and looked around. The room was scarcely six foot square, and contained no other furniture except the couch they were sitting on. In the wall in front of him was a round aperture, apparently an air-shaft. On his right he saw a dark niche. He said slowly:

'I suspected there was a secret room here near the corner of the building, but judging by the depth of the window niches in the corridor, that was impossible. There didn't seem to be enough space for one.'

'There isn't!' Sun said with a chuckle. 'But a thick supporting wall is built on the outside against the corner of this building, and this snug little room is inside that wall. You can't see it from the other side of the ravine that runs along this side of the monastery, nor can you see it from the windows of the east wing opposite. The old builders knew their job, you see! What made you think there was a secret room here, Dee?'

'Only a lucky accident,' the judge replied with a sigh. 'Last night, shortly after my arrival here, a window blew open and I got a brief glimpse of this room. I saw you while you were moving that wooden statue which you had taken from the Gallery of Horrors. I only saw your back, and I mistook the smooth grey hair plastered to your head for a close-fitting helmet. And I thought the statue was a real woman. That was the hallucination I consulted you about.'

'Well, well!' Sun said astonished. 'So you consulted me about myself, so to speak!' He laughed heartily.

'That scene,' Judge Dee continued with impassive face, 'set me chasing after the actor Mo Mo-te, who wore such an antique helmet during his sword dance. I can't understand, though, why that window on the right there doesn't show on the outside. That is the window I must have seen.'

'It is,' Sun replied. 'But it's a trick-window, you know. I can't claim any credit for it, it was there already when last year I discovered this useful little room. The shutters are, as you see, on the inside, and the panels of oiled paper on the outside are flush with the surface of the wall, and painted like bricks. Transparent paint was used, so that one can open the shutters at daytime and have light to see by, without any outside people noticing anything.' He pensively caressed his short ringbeard and went on: 'Yes, I remember now, last night I opened it to get some fresh air. The window is on the side away from the wind, you see. I didn't think it would do any harm, for I knew that the shutters of all the windows opposite were closed tightly because of the storm. When I heard one blow open, I quickly closed mine, but apparently I wasn't quick enough! I was a bit careless there, I fear!'

'You were even more careless when, during your explanation of the diagram in your library, you stated that the circle of the two forces is always divided vertically. I knew for certain that I had seen somewhere the circle depicted with a horizontal dividing line, but at that moment I didn't remember where and when that had been. If you had then told me that the circle might be represented in varying positions, I would have dismissed the subject from my mind, and forgotten all about it.'

Sun hit his hand on his knee. He said with a smile:

'Yes, now I remember you asking about that. I must confess that I hadn't thought at all about the secret lock when I was giving you my explanation. You are an observant fellow, Dee! But how did you manage to turn the disk round? It screws a vertical bar up and down along the side of the door, and it doesn't turn easily. There's a special key for it, you know!' He took from his bosom an iron hook with two protruding teeth and a long handle. The judge saw that the teeth would fit the two holes in the disk.

'I found that my hair-needle did as well,' he said. 'It only takes more time, of course. But to come back to our subject. I think you were careless a third time when you placed Miss Kang in the Gallery of Horrors. She couldn't move her head or body, and the black paint on her hands and feet was a clever device, but with all these people about here, there was still a great risk that she would be discovered.'

'No,' Sun said reprovingly, 'there you are completely wrong, Dee. Ordinarily there wouldn't have been any risk; the gallery is closed this time of the year. And it was a very original idea don't you think? I presume the girl would have become quite amenable after passing one night there. I'll repeat the experiment, some day. Though painting her was quite a job, I'll tell you! But I like to do things well. You are an enterprising fellow, Dee. The deduction from the cat's eyes was quite clever of you. I had overlooked that clue when I suggested to our poor friend True Wisdom how he could eliminate the old Abbot. True Wisdom, I regret to say, was really a mean person, only out for wealth and power, but lacking the initiative and will-power for acquiring all that by himself. When he was still the Prior here, he once stole a large sum of money from the monastery's treasury. He would have been done for if I had not helped him. Therefore he was obliged to help me with my own little pastimes! The old Abbot now, that was another man for you! Clever as they make them! Fortunately he was getting on in years, and when he found out that something was going on with those girls here he immediately suspected True Wisdom – that poor fish who didn't even know what a woman looks like! I found it safer to instruct True Wisdom to do away with old Jade Mirror, and I persuaded the Chief Abbot in the capital to appoint True Wisdom as successor.'

Sun pensively pulled at his ragged eyebrows. Giving Judge Dee a shrewd look he went on:

'True Wisdom had become rattled, of late. He kept worrying about the insinuations made by that rascally poet, and he also maintained that a strange monk had wormed his way into this monastery and was spying on him. It was a fellow with a morose face. True Wisdom thought he had seen him somewhere before. Presumably the same fellow you were after, Dee! All nonsense, of course. Just before your arrival I had to take True Wisdom up to my attic and give him a good talking to. But it didn't help, apparently. He was steadily losing his head, that's why the fool tried to kill you. He badly bungled that – I am glad to say.'

The judge remained silent. He thought for a while, then said:

'No, True Wisdom's fears of that morose monk were well founded. Where did you find that girl

176

called Liu who died here while you were treating her for a lingering disease?'

'Lingering disease is a most appropriate term!' Sun said with a chuckle. 'Well, Miss Liu was something quite special, Dee. A strong, well-developed girl, and lots of spirit! She was a member of a band of vagabonds, and got arrested while stealing chickens from a farm outside the capital. My good Mrs Pao got her by bribing the prison guards.'

'I see. That morose monk, as you call him, was Miss Liu's brother. I was told that his real name might be Liu. At times he went about as a vagrant Taoist monk, and in that role he had visited this monastery before. He suspected that his sister had been murdered here. He came back in the guise of the actor Mo Mo-te, in order to find the murderer and to avenge her death. The Abbot was quite right in worrying about Mo, he is a splendid swordsman, and you know how particular those gangs are with regard to settling blood-feuds.'

'Well,' Sun said indifferently, 'the Abbot is dead and gone, and we'll blame everything on him, so your bellicose Mr Mo will be satisfied. My friend True Wisdom made a sad mistake, though, when at the last moment he wanted to denounce me to you, hoping thereby to save his own skin.'

Judge Dee nodded. He said:

'The Abbot didn't commit suicide, of course. I ought to have suspected that at once. You pushed him from the landing, didn't you!'

'That's true!' Sun said happily. 'I thought I

177

showed great presence of mind on that occasion! I was quite impressed by your reasoning, Dee! It was so logical that I myself nearly began to believe that he had indeed committed suicide! Listen, I am sorry I can't offer you a cup of tea. That is unfortunately not included in the facilities of this cosy little room!'

'Did you have other helpers here besides the Abbot and Mrs Pao?'

'Of course not! As an experienced magistrate you'll know very well, Dee, that if you want to keep something secret, you shouldn't rope in all the world and his wife!'

'I suppose you killed Mrs Pao here?' the judge asked, looking at the blood-stained chopper on the floor.

'Yes, I could take no chances with her, after I had found the gallery open and Miss Kang gone. Killing her presented no problem of course, but I had to do some hard work to get her remains through that air-shaft over there; she was a portly woman, you know. But her pieces will rest in peace, if you'll allow me a feeble pun! At the bottom of the ravine is a cleft; nobody has yet succeeded in exploring its depths. I somewhat regret the loss of Mrs Pao, though, for she made herself quite useful, and I had built up an excellent reputation for her in the capital. But the pious widow had to go, for she was the only one who could testify against me after you had wrecked my plans with little Miss Kang.' He added with a quick smile: 'Don't think I hold that against you,

Dee! I enjoy a battle of wits with a clever opponent like you. You are doubtless a fine chess player. Let's have a game tomorrow. You do play chess don't you?'

'Hardly,' Judge Dee replied. 'My favourite game is dominoes.'

'Dominoes, eh?' Sun said disappointed. 'Well, I won't quarrel with another man's tastes. As regards Mrs Pao, I'll soon find another woman who'll continue her pious work.'

'Mrs Pao was indeed an important witness,' the judge said slowly. He caressed his sidewhiskers, looking pensively at his host. Then he resumed:

'Tell me, why did you leave the capital and settle down in this lonely monastery?'

A reminiscent smile curved Sun's lips. He patted the silvery locks on his large round head and replied:

'When I had the signal honour of explaining to His Majesty the Taoist creed, a few courtiers and Palace ladies became interested in the secret rites. I found the daughter of a certain chamberlain rather attractive, and she was so enthusiastic! Unfortunately the stupid wench killed herself. It was all hushed up, of course, but I had to leave the Palace. I found this monastery a suitable place for continuing my studies. Mrs Pao got three girls to keep me company during the past year, quite satisfactory ones. Unfortunately all of them died, as you doubtless know.'

'What did really happen to the girl who fell

from the tower above us here – by accident, as it was said?'

'She didn't go up to the tower at all! At least not on the day she died. She had been to my special room up there, of course. You should see it, Dee, it's all draped with yellow brocade! Miss Kang was quite impressed, I think. But, to come back to the other one, Miss Gao, as she was called. She went the same way as Mrs Pao just now, but of her own free will, mind you. I had put her in this room here, and chose to forget about her for a day or so, to teach her a lesson. She succeeded in wriggling through that narrow air-shaft there. She was quite a slender girl, you see.'

'If you confess as readily in my tribunal as you do now,' Judge Dee said dryly, 'you'll make things very easy for me.'

Sun raised his tufted eyebrows.

'In the tribunal?' he asked, astonished. 'What on earth are you talking about, Dee?'

'Well,' the judge replied, 'you committed five murders, not to speak of rape and abduction. You weren't thinking I would let you get away with that, were you?'

'My dear fellow!' Sun exclaimed. 'Of course you'll let me get away with it – if you insist on using that vulgar expression. Your only witnesses against me were our good Abbot and Mrs Pao – and neither of them is with us any more. After the instructive experiences I had with the two girls in the old Abbot's time, I never showed myself before the girls were completely under control. All

180

the blame for the treatment Miss Kang underwent will go to True Wisdom and Mrs Pao.' As Judge Dee shook his head emphatically, Sun exclaimed: 'Come now, Dee, I think you are a clever man, don't disappoint me! Of course you could never initiate a case against me. What would the higher authorities think if you accused me, the famous Taoist sage and former Imperial Tutor Sun Ming, of a string of fantastic crimes, and that without a shred of proof? Everybody would think you had gone raving mad, Dee. It would break your career! And I would be genuinely sorry for that, for I really like you, you know!'

'And if, in order to substantiate my case, I referred to that unsavoury affair in the Palace you just told me about?'

Sun Ming laughed heartily.

'My dear Dee, don't you realize that the said little mishap is a closely guarded Palace secret, involving most illustrious names? As soon as you breathed one word about that, you would find yourself demoted and sent to a far-away place – if they didn't put you in jail, in solitary confinement for the rest of your life!'

Judge Dee thought for a while, slowly stroking his beard.

'Yes,' he said with a sigh, 'I am afraid that you are quite right.'

'Of course I am right! I quite enjoyed this conversation, it's nice to be able to discuss one's hobbies with such an understanding person as you. But I must ask you to forget all about this, Dee.

You'll return to Han-yuan with the personal satisfaction that you solved for yourself some knotty problems, and got the better of me in the case of little Miss Kang. And I'll continue my peaceful life here in the monastery. Of course you won't try to restrain, either directly or indirectly, my future activities, you are much too clever for that – you are doubtless aware of the fact that I still have considerable influence in the capital. You have now learned the valuable lesson, Dee, that law and custom are only there for the common people, they don't apply to exalted persons like me. I belong to that small group of chosen people, Dee, who, because of their superior knowledge and talents, are far above ordinary human rules and limitations. We have advanced beyond such conventional notions as "good" and "bad". If the storm destroys a house and kills all the inmates, you don't summon the storm to your tribunal, do you? Well, this lesson you'll find very useful later, Dee, when you have been appointed to a high post in the capital, as doubtless you will be. Then you'll remember this conversation, and you'll be grateful to me!' He rose and clapped the judge on his shoulder. 'We'll go down to the hall now,' he added briskly. 'The monks'll be starting the preparations for breakfast by and by. This mess I'll clean up later. First of all we need a good meal. Both of us had rather a strenuous night, I dare say!'

Judge Dee got up also.

'Yes,' he said wearily, 'let's go down.' Noticing

that Sun was going to take his wide cloak he said politely: 'Allow me to carry that for you, sir. The weather has cleared.'

'Thank you!' Sun said, handing him the cloak. 'Yes, it's funny with these mountain storms, they'll start suddenly, rage for a time with incredible vehemence, then as suddenly subside. I don't complain, though, as they occur only at this time of the year. Generally the climate here suits me very well.'

Judge Dee took up the lantern. They passed through the cupboard. As Sun turned the disk to close the secret door he said over his shoulder: 'I don't think I need to change this lock, Dee! There aren't many persons like you who are observant enough to notice that the design of the Two Forces is in an unusual position!'

Silently they walked through the corridor, then descended a steep flight of steps that brought them to the portal of the temple. Sun looked outside and said with satisfaction:

'Yes, it is indeed dry now and the wind had gone down. We can walk to the refectory across the courtyard.'

When they were descending the steps leading down into the paved court, grey in the morning twilight, Judge Dee asked:

'What did you use that other secret room for, sir? Up there, above the store-room? I saw a small round window there, barely visible. Or shouldn't I ask that?'

Sun halted in his steps.

'You don't say!' he exclaimed astonished. 'I never knew about that one. Those ancient architects were up to all kinds of tricks. You are a useful fellow to have around, Dee! Show me where you saw that window!'

Judge Dee took him over to the high gate that closed the space between the east wing and the building of the store-room. He put the lantern and the cloak on the ground, lifted the heavy crossbeam from the iron hooks, and pulled the door open. When Sun had gone inside, Judge Dee stepped back and closed the door. As he replaced the cross-bar he heard Sun knocking on the panel of the peep-hole. Judge Dee took up the lantern and opened it. The light shone on Sun's astonished face.

'What do you mean by that, Dee?' he asked, perplexed.

'It means that you shall be judged inside there, Sun Ming. Unfortunately you were right when you explained to me that I could never initiate a case against you in my tribunal. I therefore now leave the decision to a Higher Tribunal. Heaven shall decide whether five foul murders shall be avenged, or whether I shall perish. You have two chances, Sun, whereas your victims had none. It is quite possible that your presence there will be ignored. Or, if you are attacked, you may still be able to draw the attention of the one man that can save you.'

Sun's face grew purple with rage.

'One man you say, you conceited fool? In an

hour or so there'll be scores of monks about in the yard; they'll set me free at once!'

'They'll certainly do so – if you are then still alive,' the judge said gravely. 'There is something with you in there.'

Sun looked round. Indistinct sounds came from the darkness.

He grabbed the bars of the peep-hole. Pressing his distorted face close to them he shouted frantically:

'What is that, Dee?'

'You'll find out,' the judge said. He shut the panel.

As he entered the temple building again, a scream of terror rent the air.

20

Judge Dee slowly climbed the stairs to the landing over the temple. There was still no sign of Tao Gan. He went into the corridor leading to the store-room and opened the second window on his right. Deep down below he heard weak moans, mixed with angry growling. Then there were dry, snapping sounds as of dead branches breaking. He raised his eyes to the windows in the guest-building opposite. All of them remained as they were, the shutters securely closed. He heaved a deep sigh. The case had been decided.

He laid Sun's cloak on the low window-sill, then quickly turned away. After breakfast he would draw up the document about Sun's accidental death, occurring when he leaned too far out of the low window while watching the bear down below.

With a sigh he retraced his steps to the landing. He heard quick footsteps, then saw Tao Gan, who came rushing round the corner. His lieutenant said with a contented smile:

'I was just going to look for you, sir! You needn't search for Mo Mo-te. I have got him!'

He took the judge to the next corridor. A powerfully-built man clad in a monk's cowl was lying unconscious on the floor, with his hands and feet securely tied. Judge Dee stooped and held his lantern close. He recognized the morose face. This was the tall, sullen man he had met in the storeroom, together with the elder monk whom he had asked whether Mo had been there.

'Where did you find him?' he asked, righting himself.

'Soon after Your Honour had gone up to Master Sun's library, I saw him sneaking up here. I followed him, but he is a wily customer. It took me quite some time before I could come up behind him close enough to throw my thin noose of waxthread over his head. I pulled it tight till he passed out, then trussed him up neatly.'

'You'd better untruss him again!' Judge Dee said wryly. 'He's not our man. I was wrong about him all along. His real name is Liu, he and his sister were members of a gang of vagabonds. But he also works on his own, sometimes as a Taoist mendicant monk, sometimes as an actor. He is probably a rough-and-ready rascal, but he came here for a laudable purpose, namely to avenge the murder of his sister. When you have freed him, come and sit down with me on the landing. I am tired.'

He turned round and walked back to the landing, leaving Tao Gan standing there, dumbfounded. Judge Dee sat down on the wooden bench and let his head lean back against the wall.

When Tao Gan came, the Judge pointed to the place by his side. Sitting there together in the semi-darkness, he told Tao Gan about his discovery of the secret room and his conversation with Sun Ming. He said in conclusion:

'I don't blame myself for not realizing earlier that I had mistaken Sun's round head with the smooth silvery hair for that of a soldier wearing a close-fitting iron helmet. There was no reason for connecting a man of Sun's eminence and supposed integrity with such sordid crimes. But I ought to have begun suspecting him as soon as True Wisdom had admitted his guilt, and thereby confirmed that there had indeed been irregularities with women in this monastery.'

Tao Gan looked puzzled. After a while he asked:

'Why should that have aroused suspicions regarding Master Sun, sir?'

'I ought then to have realized, Tao Gan, that a man of Sun's intelligence and experience could not have failed to notice that queer things were going on here. I should have suspected him all the more since, when I talked with him just after True Wisdom's death, Sun stressed that he always stayed in his library and used to keep himself aloof from all that went on in the monastery. I should have remembered then that True Wisdom had assured me during our first interview that Sun, on the contrary, had always shown a lively interest in all the affairs of the monastery. And that should have suggested to me at once that Sun was implicated in the murders, that the Abbot wanted to denounce him as an accomplice, and that, therefore, Sun pushed him from the landing. When, directly thereafter, we were drinking tea with Tsung Lee in the temple hall, I had a vague feeling that there was something wrong somewhere, but I failed to discover the truth. I needed a broken saucer to see all the facts in their proper connexion!'

The judge heaved a deep sigh, and slowly shook his head. Then he yawned and continued:

'Taoism penetrates deep into the mysteries of life and death, but its abstruse knowledge may inspire that evil, inhuman pride that turns a man into a cruel fiend. And its profound philosophy about balancing the male and female elements may degenerate to those unspeakable rites with women. The question is, Tao Gan, whether we are meant to discover the mystery of life, and whether that discovery would make us happier. Taoism has many elevated thoughts, it teaches us to requite good with good, and bad also with good. But the instruction to requite bad with good belongs to a better age than we are living in now, Tao Gan! It's a dream of the future, a beautiful dream – yet only a dream. I prefer to keep to the practical wisdom of our Master Confucius, who teaches us our simple, everyday duties to our fellow-men and to our society, and to requite good with good, and bad with justice!' After a while he resumed: 'Of course it would be foolish to ignore entirely the existence of mysterious, supernatural phenomena. Yet most occurrences which we consider as such prove in the end to have a perfectly natural explanation. When I was in the passage where you have now deposited Mo, I heard my name whispered. I remembered the weird story about the ghosts of the slaughtered people, and thought that it was a warning that I was about to die. However, when, thereafter, I entered the storeroom, I found there Mo Mo-te and another monk, a confederate of his, who apparently helped him to change from his warrior's costume into an old monk's cowl they had taken from a box there. I now realize that those two must have been talking about me, and a queer effect of the echo made me overhear them in the next corridor.'

'That's right!' a hoarse voice spoke up. 'My friend said I should report my sister's murder to you. But I know better. You smug officials won't lift a finger for us, the common people!'

The hulking shape of Mo Mo-te stood before them.

Judge Dee looked up at the threatening figure.

'You ought to have followed your friend's advice,' he said evenly. 'You would have saved yourself much trouble. And me too.'

Mo scowled at him, fingering the red weal round his throat. Then he stepped up close to the judge. Bending over him he growled:

'Who killed my sister?'

'I found the murderer,' Judge Dee replied curtly. 'He confessed, and I sentenced him to death. Your sister has been avenged. That's all you need to know.'

Quick as lightning Mo pulled a long knife from his bosom. Keeping it poised expertly at Judge Dee's throat, he hissed:

'Tell me or you are done for! It's me who shall kill her murderer! I am her brother. And what are you, eh?'

Judge Dee folded his arms in his sleeves. Looking up at Mo with his burning eyes, he said slowly:

'I represent the law, Mo. It's I who take vengeance.' Lowering his gaze he added in a voice that was suddenly utterly tired: 'And it is I who shall answer for it.'

He closed his eyes and leaned his head against the wall again.

Mo glared at Judge Dee's pale, impassive face. His large hand tightened on the hilt of the knife until the knuckles stood out white. Sweat began to pearl on his low forehead, his breathing came heavily. Tao Gan looked tensely at the hand with the knife.

Then Mo averted his blazing eyes. He gave Tao Gan a sombre glance, put the knife back in his bosom and said, sullenly:

'Then I have nothing to seek here any more.'

He turned round and walked unsteadily to the stairs.

After a while Judge Dee opened his eyes. He said in a toneless voice:

'Forget all I told you about Sun Ming and his crimes, Tao Gan. We keep to the story that it was the Abbot and Mrs Pao who maltreated and killed those three girls and tortured Miss Kang. Sun died by an unfortunate accident. He is survived by three sons, and we must not wantonly destroy

191

other people's lives. Too many already do their utmost to destroy their own, all by themselves!'

For a long time the judge and his lieutenant sat there together, silently listening to the chant that came up to them from the temple hall below, punctuated by beats on a wooden gong – the monks at the Abbot's bier were still reciting the prayers for the dead. Judge Dee could make out the words of the refrain, repeated with monotonous insistence:

'To die is to return home
Returning home to one's father's house,
The drop that regains the stream,
The large stream that flows on for ever.'

At last Judge Dee rose. He said:

'Go now to the store-room and fix the secret lock so that it can't work. The secret room only contains the old statue of the naked woman, and I shall forbid having naked women exposed in the Gallery of Horrors anyway. That secret room shall never again tempt anyone to commit deeds of evil! We'll meet after breakfast!'

He went with Tao Gan as far as the first window in the corridor, where he had deposited Sun's cloak as evidence of the accident. While Tao Gan went on he opened the shutters wide.

All was quiet deep down below. Suddenly a dark shape swooped down into the space between the two buildings, followed by another. The mountain vultures had discovered a prey.

Judge Dee went back to the landing and descended the stairs leading down to the temple hall. When he stepped out on the open platform in front of the temple gate he looked up. The red rays of dawn were streaking the grey sky.

He went down the broad steps, then headed for the main entrance of the east wing. While passing the high gate that closed off the well between the east wing and the building he had just left, he suddenly stood still. He stared at a hand that held on to the top of the gate with blood-stained, broken fingers. For one brief moment he thought that Sun was hanging there on the other side, in a last frantic attempt to escape. But then a vulture came down, picked up the hand and flew away towards the mountains.

Slowly the judge climbed the stairs leading up to the third floor. Every step hurt him and his back was aching. He had to rest a while on each landing. When at last he knocked on the door of his own quarters, he was swaying on his feet.

In the dressing-room the maids were busy fanning the coals in the brazier, heating the morning rice.

When he entered the bedroom he found that his three wives had just risen. The window curtains were still drawn, and in the dim light of the candles the room was cosy and warm. The First Lady sat with bare torso by the dressing-table, and the two others, still in their bed-robes, were helping her to do her hair.

Judge Dee sat down heavily at the small tea-table. He took off his cap, removed the bandage and felt the bruised spot. As he carefully replaced his cap, his third wife gave him a searching look and asked anxiously:

'I hope that my bandage helped?'

'It most certainly did!' the judge replied with feeling.

'I knew it would!' she said happily. Handing him a cup of steaming tea she added: 'I'll draw the curtains and open the shutters. I hope the storm has blown over.'

Slowly sipping his tea, the judge followed his First Lady's graceful movements as she combed her long tresses, looking intently into the round mirror of polished silver that his second wife held up for her. He passed his hand over his eyes. In these peaceful surroundings the horrors of the past night suddenly seemed nothing but a weird nightmare.

His First Lady gave her hair a final pat. She thanked the other who had been assisting her. Pulling her bed-robe up round her bare shoulders she came over to the tea-table and wished the judge a good morning. Noticing his haggard face she exclaimed:

'You look all done in! What on earth have you been at all night? I saw you come in once to take things from our medicine chest. Has there been an accident?'

'A person fell ill,' Judge Dee replied vaguely, 'and we needed some drugs. Then there were a few odds and ends that had to be attended to. Now everything has been straightened out.'

'You shouldn't have been gadding about all night, and that with your cold!' she said reprovingly. 'Well, I'll quickly make you a nice bowl of hot gruel, that'll do you good!' Passing by the open window she looked out and added briskly: 'We'll have a pleasant trip back to Han-yuan. It's going to be a beautiful day!'

Judge Dee and his Three Wives

Postscript

Judge Dee was a historical person who lived from A.D. 630 to 700. In the earlier part of his career, when he was serving as magistrate in various country districts, he earned fame as a detector of crimes; and later, after he had been appointed at Court, he proved to be a brilliant statesman who greatly influenced the internal and foreign policies of the Tang Empire. The adventures related here, however, are entirely fictitious, although many features were suggested by original old Chinese sources. The clue of the cat's eyes, for instance, I borrowed from an anecdote told about the Sung-scholar and artist Ou-yang Hsiu (A.D. 1007–1072); he possessed an old painting of a cat among peonies, and pointed out that it must have been painted at noon, because the flowers were wilting and the cat's pupils mere slits.

The Chinese professed three creeds, Confucianism, Taoism and Buddhism, the last having been introduced from India in the first century A.D. Since old Chinese detective and crime stories were written in the main by Confucianist scholars, that literature evinces a pronounced partiality to Confucianism, a feature which I adopted also in my Judge Dee novels. The characterization of Confucianist and Taoist ideals given in the present novel is based on authentic Chinese texts.

The plates I drew in the style of sixteenth-century Chinese illustrated blockprints, especially the fine Ming edition of the *Lieh-nü-chuan* 'Biographies of Illustrious Women'. Those plates represent, therefore, costumes and customs of the Ming period, rather than those of the Tang dynasty. Note that in Judge Dee's time the Chinese did not wear pigtails; that custom was imposed on them after A.D. 1644, when the Manchus had conquered China. The men did their long hair up in a top-knot, and wore caps both inside and outside the house. Tobacco and opium were introduced into China many centuries later.

7-vii-1961
Robert van Gulik